Shadow Over Scorpio

Shadow Over Scorpio

Juanita Coulson

Five Star • Waterville, Maine

First Edition
First Printing: April 2004

Published in 2004 in conjunction with Tekno Books
and Ed Gorman.

Set in 11 pt. Plantin by Christina S. Huff.

Printed in the United States on permanent paper.

ISBN 1-59414-200-9 (hc : alk. paper)

Dedication

Bruce Coulson
and
Steve Ringley
Without whom . . .

Chapter 1

Holly placed the remaining dishes in a box and glanced around the nearly empty kitchen. She felt a brief pang of regret, but no more than that. The past year had eclipsed nearly every pleasant memory associated with this house. Grief had been burned out of her. Dead and gone, like the man so recently in his grave.

"About ready, Pet?" Bianca called from the next room. Without waiting for a reply, her older sister continued her phone conversation. Holly heard her arranging for a local charity to collect the remaining furnishings and kitchenware. Finishing that task, Bianca repeated more loudly, "Ready, Pet?"

Moving slowly, Holly went to the door between the rooms and said through gritted teeth, "Don't call me that. You know how I hate that nickname."

Bianca's eyes widened, as though she'd received shocking news. That reaction annoyed Holly almost as much as Bianca's use of the nickname. "Oh, Pet . . . Holly, I'm sorry. I forgot. It's just that . . . old habits die hard, you know?" Paling, Bianca clasped a beautifully manicured hand across her mouth. "Oh! I . . . I shouldn't have said that, should I? I don't know what made me do it." She shuddered and looked uneasily at the old furniture pushed against the walls. "It's . . . it seems so unreal. Him being—"

"Dead," Holly said in a flat tone. "It's quite real enough to me—after taking care of him for almost a year. His death was

7

indeed the blessed relief the religious texts speak of, for both of us."

"Holly! How can you say such a thing?"

"Don't you think I have the right? You weren't here, except for a few rare visits."

"He was so . . ."

"Difficult? But that wasn't anything new, was it? He always was proud and stubborn, set on making his own way in the world without any outside help. But then the disease made that impossible. And when his body and mind began failing, he took out his resentment on his caretaker. Me. Well, that's what I expected would happen. I prepared myself for it." Holly slumped onto the arm of the well-worn sofa and went on sourly, "I knew what I was getting into, so I shouldn't complain, right? He'd assigned our roles when we were kids, and I guess we never outgrew those. You were his free spirit and I was the obedient good little girl. So, naturally, when everything started going to hell, I played my part—enduring his worsening moods and rages and unreasonable demands . . ."

"He *could* be kind and sweet and fun." Bianca said with considerable heat. "You *know* he could!"

For a long moment, the sisters stared at each other. Finally, Holly shrugged and sighed. "Yes, he could. That was the worst of it. Occasionally that sweet part of his personality would resurface, just for a little while. But the moments never lasted. He hated what was happening to him, and there was absolutely nothing anyone could do to stop it. He wanted to kick fate, but fate wasn't available. So he took his anger out on me, and sometimes apologized afterward. Sometimes. Meanwhile, you . . ."

Bianca's chin went up and her lovely grey eyes flashed. "*I* was paying the bills. All of them. And they weren't small. Remember that."

With a nod, Holly sighed again and said, "Yes, you were. Okay. I'll shut up. I had a lot of practice doing that during this past year."

"Will you stop it?" her sister exclaimed, exasperated. "I *told* you I'll make it up to you. Stephen and I both will. It's . . . it's terrible, sure, that you had to quit your job at the college to . . . to become his nurse. But that's all over now. Everything is going to change. You'll see! Oh, please! Let's don't quarrel. Why do we always have to quarrel?"

It was on the tip of Holly's tongue to retort: *"Because you're the beautiful, successful big sister. And I'm Little Miss Practical, as Dad tended to call me. Just as you call me 'Pet,' and there are times when I think that's exactly what I am to you . . ."*

Instead, she took a deep breath and said calmly, "All right. It's just . . . I suppose I'm feeling somewhat guilty. I barely mustered enough tears at the funeral to be decent. The only thing I could think was—now he isn't suffering any longer."

Bianca laid a hand on her arm. "As you've said, it's not as if he had anything to live for. You stood by him all these months . . ."

"Someone had to." Her sister blushed at that remark, and Holly felt a perverse urge to apologize for opening fresh wounds.

"Okay, okay! I had that coming," Bianca said, adopting a theatrical manner. "I admit it. I've been a selfish bitch. But try to put yourself in my shoes for a moment . . ." When she saw Holly's expression, she rushed on, "Don't think it didn't tear me to pieces, knowing you were trapped here, that I was getting the goodies and you the crumbs. There! You see? I can be completely honest, can't I? That's Stephen's doing. He's made all the difference in the world. And he'll help me make a difference for you, too, Pet. We might even have done something for Father—"

"Nobody could have done anything for him," Holly cut in angrily. "The disease wasn't curable. I explained that to you again and again . . ."

"Yes, yes, I know. I'm sorry. Please, be patient with me."

The words took Holly aback. Bianca, being humble? Maybe her new husband was indeed the miracle-worker Bianca kept saying he was. Her older sister actually had the grace to look contrite, and it didn't seem to be the sort of act she'd adopted so many times as a child. Was it possible a whirlwind courtship and marriage to a world-famous celebrity had mellowed her lifelong me-first attitude?

Bianca stared around the room with sudden loathing. "I swear to God, I was going to move the two of you out of this rat trap, get a full-time nurse for Father, set it all up. Stephen has that kind of money. He suggested it. Why did Father have to die *now?* Just when I had everything in my hands?"

She shook her head violently, her dark coppery hair brushing the shoulders of her couture suit with every motion. She might have been on a stage, putting on a dramatic performance of frustrated grief.

And yet . . . Holly sensed that *this* time Bianca's words were sincere. Impulsively, she brushed her sister's cheek with gentle fingertips, as she used to do when they were both children. "Don't let it eat at you. He's dead. Let him, and us, rest in peace."

Bianca's smile was the sun emerging from storm clouds. She embraced Holly, and cried, "Oh, yes. Let's go. I can't wait to get out of here, to get you home, where Stephen and I can make it all right. You'll just love Stephen!"

"Your paragon," Holly said with a wry smile, remembering the phrase from the blizzard of Bianca's phone calls during the recent courtship.

"He is! When you meet him you'll see exactly what I

mean. I'm such a selfish, conceited bitch, I know, I know! But during these last few heavenly weeks, my magnificent Scorpio has completely changed my life direction. I couldn't imagine coming here instead of flying to Spain with him on that business trip. But he absolutely insisted. It was my duty, he said. He *knew* I had to come here to be with you."

Holly wondered if her new brother-in-law realized the irony in that situation. Bianca had indeed paid the bills, but she'd almost never visited during this final, horrible year of their father's life. And now, after a week of living once more under the same roof with this stranger who was her sister, that irony was all the more keen. Bianca's sudden arrival here for the funeral seemed . . . vulturish. In at the kill, when she'd pointedly avoided all the emotional and physical struggles preceding Father's death.

"I wish I could have attended the wedding." Bianca colored under her deep, luscious tan, and Holly went on lamely. "I mean . . . I know it was very impulsive. An elopement . . ."

"You can't imagine the circus it would have been if the paparazzi had found out about it," her sister said. Then she peered around the house again and shivered. "Do you want to hang around any longer? Anyone you want to say good-bye to?"

"Not really. I said it all at the funeral. Let's leave. The sooner the better."

"A fresh start!" Bianca enthused. They picked up Holly's discount store suitcases and headed for the door. As they left, Holly closed that door behind her very firmly.

A next-door neighbor and her father's closest friend stood by Bianca's sporty car. Both senior citizens nodded sympathetically as the women approached. Holly responded absently to their condolences. The men insisted on loading her cases in the trunk, carefully packing the luggage between two small boxes of photos and other memorabilia that Holly couldn't bear to leave behind.

"I guess you girls are ready to go now?"

"Yes, and thanks for all you've done, Mr. Johnson." Holly had long since become expert at these homey exchanges with her father's war buddies and cronies. "Were you able to dispose of the car?"

"Sure did. Got fifty dollars for it."

"For that junker?" Holly said with genuine surprise. "I thought we'd have to pay someone to take it away. You're a good salesman, and an even better realtor, I'm sure." She fished in her purse for the house keys and handed them to Mr. Johnson. "The charity people will be here later today. So don't lock up until they've gone, please. I really do appreciate you taking care of all this."

Johnson waved his hand dismissively. "Don't you worry none. It's a nice little house. Won't have no trouble at all selling it." He went on doubtfully, "Sure you don't want to hang onto it for a while? Place to stay when you come back to visit."

Holly shook her head, swallowing an urge to blurt out that she had no intention of ever returning to Norris Falls. "N . . . no, I'll be staying with Bianca and her husband until I . . . until I decide what I want to do. Uh . . . when I stop by here again, I'll probably . . . oh, rent an apartment."

Johnson patted her hand solicitously and repeated, "Don't you worry none." He eyed Bianca thoughtfully, as if unsure this glamorous creature was indeed the pretty little girl with pigtails he remembered from earlier days. Returning his attention to Holly, he asked, "Now, have I got your new address right? Care of Mr. Stephen Detloff, Scorpio House, Dark Lake?" She nodded and he went on, "You'll be hearin' from me real soon about the house. I'll tidy things up just the way Bill woulda wanted me to."

Holly murmured her appreciation yet again, anxious to get away. Johnson was a good, kindly man. He'd been infinitely patient throughout her father's many ugly moods, enduring much for the sake of a comradeship forged in a terrible war. She knew the man was totally honest and conscientious, and she could safely leave the shards of her former life in his hands.

"Well, we'd better be going," she said, trying to sound reluctant.

"Right. Long trip and a hot day, but I imagine you've got AC in this nice little buggy." Johnson bustled about, helping both women into the car. Bianca flashed him a dazzling smile as he closed her door.

"I'll write, or e-mail you, as soon as I get settled," Holly promised, speaking loudly as the car's engine roared to life. Then her sister touched a button and the windows closed, shutting off further conversation. Inwardly, Holly was grateful for the noise and the glass wall, sparing her the need to exchange any more drawn-out courtesies.

As Bianca drove through Norris Falls, the former fashion model didn't bother to hide her true feelings. "Good God! I'd forgotten what a stodgy, frozen-in-amber little drinkwater burg this is! It's a good thing we're getting you away from here before you stagnate completely. Besides, Stephen says it's best that you be with us when . . ." She stopped abruptly and focused all her attention on the road.

"When what?" Holly demanded, puzzled by her sister's sudden change of mood.

"Never mind!"

Bianca sounded angry, and frightened. A chill snaked up Holly's spine. *Stephen says it's best that you be with us*

13

when . . . What on earth did *that* mean? Bianca was grimly silent, clutching the steering wheel so tightly her knuckles were white.

Holly was about to press for an answer when the Tollway entrance ramp loomed ahead. She put questions on hold, not wanting to cause any distraction. Bianca merged smoothly with heavy traffic and accelerated. It was a much, much faster rate of travel than Holly had been accustomed to for a long time; their father's junker simply hadn't been capable of this sort of speed. Holly gazed out at a flowing blur of vehicles, feeling as though she'd undergone a radical sea change. As indeed, she had! For more than a year her driving had been limited to short errands in and around Norris Falls—the pharmacy, discount store, small supermarket. Day after day, week after week, all of it grindingly predictable, and as dull as clockwork. Like her life—bound by the manners and mores of an easy going, slow-moving community. Norris Falls had been her universe, a haven. Boring, but utterly safe. Now she was being swept away from that calm milieu and carried off to an entirely different world.

Holly eyed her sister sidelong. What did she know, really, of her older sister's current life? Bianca might as well be an alien from another planet. She'd left Norris Falls more than five years ago, escaping into a career of high couture and fashion design. Ever since, she'd lived in a social stratosphere populated by sophisticates and celebrities. And then, just recently, Bianca capped her dazzling ascent by wedding an internationally famous astrologer, the much acclaimed "Consultant of the Stars," Stephen Detloff.

Conflicting emotions tore at Holly. She, too, had longed to escape Norris Falls.

She didn't scorn its citizens or lifestyle, as Bianca did. But the long ordeal of caring for their father had drained her of joy or hope. If she remained in that house, that town, her memories eventually would devour her utterly. She'd be permanently trapped.

But . . .

This was such an enormous leap into the unknown! Bianca's husband and their circle associated with the sort of celebrities Holly knew only from television and newspaper features. The idea of fitting into that exalted society daunted her. She was barely three years younger than her sister, even though, in terms of responsibility, she'd often felt years older. However, Bianca had jetted far, far beyond Holly's wildest imaginings. The former model now was quite at home among the rich and famous.

Well, it was too late to back out now, Holly acknowledged tiredly. Besides, where would she go and what would she do, if she *didn't* go with Bianca? Ten days ago, Bianca had returned for the funeral. Since then, the new "Mrs. Stephen Detloff" had taken over handling most of the necessary final details of their father's affairs. Holly had been grateful to let her assume that burden. But she began to realize she might have traded one sort of bondage for another. It hadn't actually been *her* decision to leave Norris Falls; Bianca simply stated as a given that "of course" Holly would henceforth live with her and Stephen. Holly had acquiesced with little argument. It seemed like a sensible plan. And at present, she certainly had none of her own. She'd go along for the ride and see where it took her.

Bianca turned on the car's CD player. Marshmallowy light classics wafted from the speakers. The selection clashed oddly with the thundering expressway traffic surrounding the little car. Nevertheless, the innocuous "elevator music" eased some of Holly's doubts; if this was a sample of her sister's taste, she must not be quite the worldly sophisticate Holly had assumed.

15

"Sorry the AC's so inadequate," Bianca said. "Our mechanic said it was fixed before I drove up, but it started to act up as soon as I got to Wisconsin. And naturally, there was nowhere in Norris Falls to get it repaired."

"Naturally," Holly murmured.

Her sister's enthusiasm was back in full force. "Oh, I have such big plans for you, Pet. We've got to get you out of that dowdy shell. You're really rather pretty, and you've got a good figure. But all those years in Norris Falls left you acting like a positive recluse. That will never do."

"The social opportunities *were* a bit limited there," Holly said, scowling. Bianca was oblivious to the sarcasm. Had she forgotten that her kid sister had led an active social life while in college? Just because she'd recently lacked for opportunity, that didn't mean that Holly hadn't wanted to date and keep up with the latest fashions.

Still blithely unaware of Holly's annoyance, Bianca chattered on. "Maybe get you a new hair style. And trim a few pounds—although there are plenty of men who like them stacked like you are. Oh, we're going to spin some heads, believe me, once we get you in shape!"

Holly grimaced. *"We."* She was Bianca's new toy. No, her "pet." Something to be fussed over and altered for Bianca's amusement.

"The most eligible bachelors at the lake right now are Kyle and Russ. Kyle's got everything: looks, money, and so much charm he almost doesn't know what to do with it. And Russ Graham isn't exactly a slouch, either." Bianca paused long enough to glance at her sister, seeing if Holly recognized the name. "Russ Graham. Oh, surely you've heard of him! He's Stephen's favorite artist, does all the work for Stephen's books and articles. You know how artists can be, Pet— broody as hell. But soooo attractive! And I never believed a word of that gossip. I certainly wouldn't let myself lose any sleep over it." For just a moment, however, there was a touch of uncertainty in her voice.

"Lose sleep over what gossip?" Holly asked.

But Bianca was already rattling on, mentioning a hairdresser's name. That led to a long recital of her last visit to the world-renowned stylist's salon, and all the amusing and irritating things that had happened there. That reminded her of numerous other incidents, other high-level visitations, other celebrities. Bianca referred to these without any explanation, as if assuming her sister would recognize all the names and places. Holly was a satellite, and Bianca was the sun, not bothering to translate her monologue for the benefit of a mere mortal.

Her babble became a drone in Holly's ears. She allowed it to wash over her like a hypnotist's chant. She hadn't slept well for weeks—months! Bianca's happy chatter and the barely functioning air conditioner lulled her into a doze.

Snatches of her sister's earlier remarks surfaced in her mind, flashing like blurred neon signs—bright and vaguely alarming. She *must* be with Stephen and Bianca, not alone, when . . . ? It suggested Stephen Detloff feared something unpleasant would happen to Holly. Why? That didn't make sense. She'd been a dying man's drudge, tied to a totally unexciting existence. Now she'd be a guest, at least for a while, of her sister and brother-in-law. What could possibly be menacing about that?

Names flared up in Holly's mind, fragments of Bianca's prattle. Kyle. That must be Kyle Preis, scion of a giant publishing firm. She remembered seeing the Preis imprint on the Stephen Detloff books Bianca had given her. And during recent evenings filled with Bianca's disconnected monologues, Holly had learned that Kyle Preis and his mother currently were sole owner-managers of a very successful Chicago-based corporation. Was Bianca seriously thinking of playing matchmaker? Shoving her sister into Preis's arms? What nonsense! Holly Frey would strike such a man as a bumpkin.

Another name. Russ Graham. Artist. Moody. But "sooo attractive." And Bianca had said something else about Graham. Gossip that Bianca didn't believe, and there had been an undercurrent of fascination and fear in her voice.

All of this was as wild and pointless as Father's disease-caused delusions.

A shape loomed up out of Holly's mental drifting: tall, masculine, the features in shadow. A hulking silhouette advancing toward her menacingly.

A strident blast of sound shocked her wide awake. With a stifled cry, Holly sat bolt upright, blinking, momentarily disoriented.

Gradually, she realized she'd been half-dreaming, and the noise which had startled her was nothing more than the horn of a truck zooming past Bianca's car.

When the thunder from the semi's tires faded and she could make herself heard, Bianca asked, "Are you okay, Pet? I thought you were going to jump out of your skin."

Music continued to murmur from the speakers. Traffic flowed steadily. On either side of the expressway lay a vista of housing developments, factories, and shopping centers. Perfectly mundane and unterrifying.

"I . . . I must have been dreaming," Holly said sheepishly. That menacing figure in her daymare still lingered in the back of her mind, and she shivered. With difficulty, she shook off the sensations. "I guess I fell asleep. Sorry."

"And while I was talking, too," Bianca chided, grinning to show she was only feigning outrage. "Poor Holly! You're really bushed." Her tone hinted she was commiserating with an old maid aunt, not a younger sister.

Holly wondered if she gave the impression of being that decrepit. Maybe Bianca was right; she *would* have to do something to perk up her image.

"That's all right. Go ahead. Soak up the shut-eye so you're fresh for the party."

"Party?" Holly said, baffled.

"Oh, look! There's a plaza. Let's pull over and get something to eat, so we won't have to waste time later."

Holly stifled her curiosity while Bianca went through the intricacies of exiting the Tollway and turning into the restaurant. From that point on, it was almost impossible to break into Bianca's enthusiasm, a disconnected ramble of people, places, and social events. Holly quit trying to interrupt. With half an ear, she listened and ate and watched the constant stream of vehicles zipping silently and rapidly under the glassed-in plaza.

"Of course, everyone puts up with Sylvia Preis. I mean, what can we do? She has so much power and money, especially since her husband died in that awful accident. Insurance, you know. We'd all love to give that woman her comeuppance, but those who've tried regret it, believe me. It's too bad, because Kyle's a real sweetie, in spite of all the tragedy he's been through. You'd think that would make a young man grim, wouldn't you? But it hasn't. Oh, and when we get to the party, be sure to admire Cynthia's prints. She has some truly spectacular finds. Besides, she's such a dear friend, she and Jason both. You know they operate one of the finest galleries in the Great Lakes area? Cynth's really opened our eyes to some of the new schools. No one had heard of some of these artists before they introduced them to the world. Oh, and I do hope Russ shows up tonight. I think it's

19

dreadful the way some people indulge in malicious slander, don't you? I mean, it's been over a year, now, and the police absolutely cleared him of any suspicion. People can be so cruel, can't they?"

Holly nodded absently and sipped her tea. There didn't seem to be any point in responding. She sat and listened to Bianca rattling on, hoping that eventually she'd learn what all of these comments referred to.

When they returned to the Tri-State Tollway, angling steadily eastward, Holly asked, "How far have we come?"

"Oh, far better than halfway." Bianca waved at a smoggy golden haze to the left. "Remember, Chicago and the Region are quite a chunk to drive around. But I didn't want to take the Dan Ryan today. I must admit that Kyle Preis always seems to make good time using it, but then he was born lucky." Bianca paused and glanced at her sister. "Is this the first time you've been down here?"

"Not quite. There were a couple of field trips, when I was a freshman in college."

"But that was . . ." She hesitated, obviously remembering the length of time that had passed since those earlier journeys, and of what had happened since. "Well, you'll get used to it, I just know you will."

Holly didn't bother to argue. As Chicago's suburbs slipped behind them, she reflected on what had been. For so long, her life had been bounded by a small Wisconsin town. "Journey" and "travel" were just words in library books and TV shows. Fifty miles from Norris Falls, a monthly trip to the VA hospital, was a grand excursion. Now she was over a hundred miles away, leaving, probably forever, the world she'd always known. And she was discovering a fact that television programs and books rarely mentioned: Travel was fatiguing.

Finally, they emerged from the miasma of the Region and

turned off I-94 into open country. Their route jogged several times—south, east, then southward again. "Just about there, Pet," Bianca said. "I know you'll love Dark Lake. Maud calls it Our Colony, our own little colony. Stephen was the very first to discover the area and build here for year-round living. Most of the residents have business ties to Chicago, of course, and this is so convenient. We don't get very many vacationers and summer trade at all." She turned onto a two-lane blacktop marked by a sign reading, "Dark Lake, Ten Miles."

"I thought Chicago commuters would prefer to live closer to Lake Michigan, or to the Dunes."

"This *is* the Dunes, Pet!" Bianca said with a laugh. "Oh, not the actual Park. But we're definitely part of the terrain, as Russ puts it. And come to that, we're barely a skip and a jump from Lake Michigan."

The northern Indiana dunes were indeed much in evidence. Sand lay banked along the roadsides and drifted around tree trunks amid patches of weeds and grass. Now and then the road curved through stretches of dense woodland or passed pastures where horses and cattle grazed.

Then the car topped a small hill and rolled down toward the sparkling expanse of a small lake. Bianca braked expertly at a sharp turn, cruising only a few yards from the breeze-chopped waters. She turned off the air conditioning and lowered the windows. Cool, delightfully refreshing lake air swept into the car. It was an exhilarating relief after the hours spent on the highway.

Holly studied the community with interest. Dark Lake was an eclectic mixture of enormous "rustic" cabins and stone-faced luxury houses. Nearly every structure boasted a manicured lawn reaching to the lake's edge, and many also featured permanent piers and boat houses. Elaborate swimmers' rafts bobbed at anchor. Everything about Dark Lake bespoke wealth, and plenty of it.

Bianca drove up a winding lane to a lushly forested hill topped by a huge rambling brick mansion. "Isn't it just too lovely?" she exclaimed. "Well, well? What do you think of Scorpio House?"

The westering sun peeked raggedly through the trees skirting the property and cast stark shadows along the east side of the mansion. Holly stared in wonder. Bianca had described this as the "throne" of Stephen Detloff's astrological empire, and everything about the place did indeed shout "Power." The dwelling was a massive three-story structure surrounded by oaks and evergreens which thickened into woods further east. Arboreal sentinels crowded close to the walls, their branches shielding Scorpio House like a group of stern-visaged soldiers clustering about their monarch.

"It's . . . very impressive," Holly finally managed, hoping that was sufficient to satisfy her sister.

The drive widened out into a miniature parking lot beside the main entrance. Bianca pulled in beside a low-slung foreign sports car. As she switched off the ignition and returned the CDs to their jewel boxes, Holly stared at the waiting mansion. A huge portico flanked double doors. Sunlight suddenly broke through clouds and reflected blindingly off the beaten brass doorplates and fittings. For a heartbeat, Holly saw it as a doorway to a pagan altar, where victims were slaughtered to feed a hungry idol.

Bianca's arm closed about her. "What's wrong, Pet?"

"N . . . nothing. It's nothing. Just a chill." Holly felt strange—ashamed of her misgivings, yet keenly alert and wary. It was as if Nature herself was lighting a beacon to warn her. Of what? And what made her feel as though a cold fist had closed around her heart?

Chapter 2

As they stepped out of the car and Holly moved toward its trunk Bianca said impatiently, "Oh, leave the suitcases and things. The servants will get those. Come on." She led the way up the broad steps.

Before they reached the top, however, the doors opened and a muscular, blond young man exited. Seeing the women, he froze. Then a charming grin split his square features. "Well, hello! You've been keeping secrets from me, Bianca. Naughty, naughty!"

Holly brushed a few stray wisps of hair back from her brow. She suspected she looked like a rumpled and sweaty mess. Not that it mattered. He surely couldn't think she'd just come out of a beauty salon.

"Pet . . . Holly, meet Kyle Preis, boy genius of the publishing world," Bianca said smoothly. "Kyle, my kid sister, Holly. She'll be a Dark Lake resident from now on. How does that suit you?"

"Need you ask?" Kyle's hazel eyes twinkled. He stared down at Holly and said, "I hope Bianca hasn't been telling you too many lies about me."

"Nothing unflattering," she responded honestly. Holly extended her hand and he wrapped it in his strong fingers. "As a matter of fact, Bianca's been telling me a great deal about everyone in her social circle here at Dark Lake."

"We'll try our best to make life interesting for you here," Kyle replied, winking broadly.

His flirtatious manner put Holly on her guard. This man was, as her sister had warned, a thoroughgoing charmer, with a lifeguard's physique and deep tan, well displayed by a white knit sport shirt and snug slacks. She suspected he had a long list of conquests to his credit—or his debit. Holly said lightly, "Is that a promise, or a threat?"

"Maybe we can make it a proposition," he came back with a toothy grin, confirming her suspicions.

"I'd rather get well settled in, first, before I think about any . . . propositions."

Kyle opened his mouth as if to bury her caution in a flood of compliments and veiled hints. Then he glanced at his watch and said, "Oh, hell! Got to run. Later, gorgeous. You, too, Bi . . ."

"Like tonight!" Bianca shouted after him as Preis ran toward the sports car.

He waved back an acknowledgment, jumped in the vehicle, and roared away. Bianca pinched Holly's arm, like a giggling schoolgirl. "Isn't he just the cutest?"

"Very, and no doubt a devil with the ladies, as Father used to say."

Heaving a sigh and shaking her head, Bianca muttered, "You are so, so right."

Holly followed her into a gigantic foyer. The interior of Scorpio House was comfortably cool and majestically impressive. Ebony furniture contrasted with startling, off-white woodwork and plush, dark red carpeting. To the right of the entrance, a curving staircase rose to the mansion's upper stories. A large archway to the left gave onto an enormous showcase living room, complete with floor-to-ceiling black velvet drapes, a flagstone fireplace, and a grand piano.

"Well? Well?" Bianca demanded, jittering with eagerness. Her intense pride and desire for approval were palpable, and completely understandable. Big sister had indeed done well for herself. She'd won it all, hadn't she? Natural beauty, a brilliant marriage, a jet-set social life, and a house worthy of a star layout in a "home beautiful" magazine or a television "rich and famous" feature.

"It's . . . spectacular," Holly admitted with awe. "Like something out of Hollywood. Your descriptions didn't do it justice—"

"Welcome back, My Own," a very deep, very masculine voice interrupted her.

Bianca whirled and cried ecstatically, "Stephen! Oh, I thought you weren't going to be back until Monday!"

A tall man was slowly descending the great staircase. He held out his long arms to enfold Bianca as she rushed into his embrace. The two kissed passionately. Holly felt embarrassed, unsure what the proper etiquette was in this circumstance. Should she avert her eyes? Turn away? Pretend she didn't see the happy lovers?

Then she became aware that she and they weren't alone. A short, sandy-haired man dodged nimbly around the clinching couple, bestowing a brief, amused glance on them as he came on down the stairs. He held out his hand and said, "Hello. You must be Mrs. Detloff's sister. Correct? We've been expecting you. I'm Toby Carmichael, Stephen's man-of-all-computer-work. But I do lots of other things around here, including greet guests."

"I'm very glad to meet you, Mr. Carmichael."

"Toby," he corrected her gently.

She nodded, studying him, since it gave her someplace else to look other than at the passionate pair steaming up the staircase. Carmichael appeared to be in his mid to late thirties. He had the sort of face that was often described as elfin, though lines in his features hinted at past tragedy. Despite that, his general manner was cheerful. He chuckled as he jerked a thumb toward Stephen and Bianca and said, "Never guess they're newlyweds, would you? Luggage still in the car?"

"Er . . . yes," Holly said, jarred by his sudden shift of topic. "Also my houseplants and a few boxes of mementoes."

"Say no more. They'll get the kid glove treatment. Clete!" he called loudly. Holly presumed "Clete" was someone who helped unload cars. She remembered Bianca's admonition and resolved to stay out of the way. Toby said, "We'll bring the stuff up the back stairs. Leave it to us. That's why we get the big bucks, eh?"

Holly wondered if he had intuitively grasped her thoughts. Such an idea was easy to accept, here in Scorpio House, with its dominating aura of the occult.

"Lovebirds will have to come up for air soon," Toby reassured her. A skinny black man came into the foyer and he and Carmichael fell into lockstep, heading for the door. "If you'll excuse us," the computer tech murmured, then went outdoors with Clete.

True to his prediction, Holly heard a sigh and turned to see that Bianca and the deep-voiced man had parted and were at last coming on down to the entryway. Bianca gazed up adoringly at her husband, her arm about his waist.

No one could fail to recognize Stephen Detloff. His portrait graced thousands of newspaper columns, magazine articles, television screens, and book dust jackets. Photos didn't capture his essence, though, in Holly's opinion. Unusually strong cheekbones and heavy brows gave him a typecast sorcerer's face. Adding to the effect, his pale skin was framed by a sleek cowl of black hair and a Mephistophelean moustache and beard. Even his physique was outside the norm—long limbs and a surprisingly short torso. It was an adolescent's gangling body, but there was nothing about Detloff to suggest callow youth. He wore a form-fitting jumpsuit of iridescent black material, accented by a pale blue ascot. Holly was almost disappointed that he didn't have a cape and carry a magic wand.

"So this is our long-awaited meeting with Holly," Stephen said, taking his sister-in-law's hands. "Ah! I would have known you for an Aquarian-Pisces cusp even if Bianca hadn't told me your birthdate. What conflicts you two must have had when you were children." It was on the tip of Holly's tongue to tell him those conflicts hadn't stopped when the children grew up, but she said nothing. "Poor Holly! Your sensible Virgo Moon would have clashed so with Bianca's Aries. And an afflicted Mars, to boot, for both of you!"

Holly's interest in astrology was minimal and quite skeptical. But Stephen's pronouncements shook her a bit. She told herself that in all likelihood he was merely a very skilled psychologist. That, and astrological jargon, enabled him to weave a spell over his listeners. Nevertheless, the man *did* radiate an aura of omniscience. She began to understand how he had won the confidence and patronage of people worldwide. He definitely qualified for that overused term, "charisma." To her surprise, Stephen bowed and kissed her hands. It was a courtly gesture she could have dismissed as mere theatricality. Yet she couldn't deny the power in his touch, as if she were coming in close contact with a dangerous, barely leashed sensual energy.

"I'm . . . very happy to meet you, Stephen."

He regarded her with deep-set, almost black eyes. "And I am profoundly sorry that we haven't met earlier. But for the three of us the opposing forces, until this very day, were insurmountable. Fate seemed to ordain that we come together now, and no sooner."

Detloff held her attention like a hypnotist. Either he was a consummate actor, or he genuinely believed everything he said about the influence of heavenly bodies. And, while he spoke, he made Holly believe, too. The man was frighteningly convincing, conjuring up images of inexorable karmic forces affecting all their lives.

"I sincerely wanted to join you, Holly, when you relayed to us the dreadful news about your father," Stephen went on apologetically. "I would have cancelled my appointments in Spain and accompanied Bianca to Norris Falls in an instant— an instant!—if it hadn't been a matter of life and death."

Bianca had mentioned that a powerful political figure recently paid a king's ransom to command Stephen's presence. All expenses covered for a consultation at a posh villa on the Mediterranean. At the time, Holly dismissed that as hyperbole. But now . . . Was it jet-set melodrama or a certified business deal? She'd read articles claiming that certain movie stars and millionaires refused to make a career move or financial investment unless an expert checked their horoscopes. Until today she hadn't really believed that.

She was tempted to tell him that events in Norris Falls had been a matter of life and death, too, but left the words unsaid. The truth was, her brother-in-law's attendance at her father's funeral wouldn't have made the slightest difference in the course of events.

"That's quite all right," Holly murmured, feeling spineless.

"I knew you would be infinitely charitable regarding others' lapses, my dear. It's that benign Saturn of yours," he said. He sounded relieved. Then he returned to his intense mode, adding, "I'm so glad you're here at last, here and safe."

Unwillingly, Holly remembered Bianca's aborted remark hours before: *Stephen says it's best that you be with us when . . .*

28

This was an opportunity to question the source of those warnings. Surely, all that was just a bad joke. It *had* to be. But once again, something made her hold her tongue.

Bianca's sudden laughter was a shower of golden coins tumbling down a velvet curtain. "I tried to warn you, Pet. Confess! You just weren't ready for Stephen, were you? Don't you think my 'Scorpio' is absolutely marvelous?"

Her sister had interpreted Holly's tongue-tied dread for admiration. Holly nodded dumbly, glad to put aside her apprehension.

Detloff didn't even blush at his wife's gushing praise. But he amended her comments. "Ah! Not quite correct, My Own. I have a Libra-Scorpio cusp, one degree into Scorpio, and I consider myself under that aegis." He turned to Holly and said, "Hence my *nom de plume*—and the name of my castle." Stephen swept a long arm wide to indicate Scorpio House, then focused his intense gaze on her again. "We are fellow cusp riders, you and I, sister of my beloved. Ah! But I swore I would not talk shop this evening!"

"Not talk shop!" Bianca exclaimed, laughing anew. "But how can you avoid it? I know you, darling. We won't be at the party five minutes before you'll have poor Jason backed into a corner, confronting him with his stellia and conjunctions."

"Brilliant man, Jason, well worth converting to the science of astrology, for all of his cynicism." Then Stephen blinked and did a double-take. He looked down at Bianca and said in a small, confused tone, "What party?" Suddenly, he was thoroughly, likeably human, a typical befuddled husband, no longer the omnipotent astrologer.

"The Martins' party. Don't you remember? They've finished their remodeling and are showing off the results. Oh, you must remember! Why, Cynthia and I sat right there in your office and made out the invitations," Bianca said. Comprehension began to dawn on Stephen's face as his wife turned to Holly. "It's fortunate Jason's such a tolerant soul. He simply can't abide astrology. And yet he allows Stephen to draw him into these endless arguments. All quite friendly, of course. Oh, you'll love Jason and Cynthia, and Maud, and Kay, and Deidre, and . . . all the rest. This will be the first big bash of the season at Dark Lake. Your timing is perfect!"

Perfect timing? Holly gaped at her sister. She acted as though their father's death and the uprooting that had followed it were inconvenient blips on a social calendar.

Then Holly realized the import of what Bianca was saying. "Do you really think it would be . . . well . . . decent? So soon after the funeral? I don't know all these people—"

"Nonsense! It'll do you a world of good. You said yourself that the grieving was over months ago. And after all, you gave Father the best care anyone possibly could. Total devotion. And there's nothing more you can do for him, now, can you? Aren't you entitled to some fun? Good God! This isn't the Middle Ages, Pet. Surely you don't intend to wear black and veil yourself for a whole year or some such idiocy!" She was a lovely juggernaut, crushing any rebuttal with sheer verbiage. "Come on! You've got to get out of that awful shell you're in. Live a little! Fresh start, no gloomy memories. Stephen, we can't let her wiggle out of it." Abruptly, she turned and shouted up the stairs, "Melanie!"

Holly's emotions were in turmoil. She glanced uneasily at Stephen. Would he veto Bianca? His reactions surprised her. While her sister continued to call for the off-stage Melanie, Detloff extracted a circular object from a breast pocket of his jumpsuit.

Holly cocked her head curiously, trying to figure out what he was holding. She saw it was some sort of calculator. For a few seconds Stephen pressed buttons, frowning. An odd expression crossed his striking features; he looked torn between worry and amusement. "Holly?" His voice was an anxious whisper.

"Melanie!"

Above them, a middle-aged black woman leaned over the upstairs railing. "Yes, Mrs. Detloff?"

"Please lay out the Lauritz chiffon, and the amethyst, will you?"

"Right away."

Holly blotted out that exchange, her attention on Stephen. A tingle of alarm gnawed at the pulse in her throat. "Y . . . yes? What is it?"

"You mustn't be afraid," he said in a sepulchral tone. "Be bold and confident, my dear. But . . . I do want to talk privately some time. It's crucial. Tomorrow, perhaps? Please? Toby will arrange my schedule to—"

"Stephen," Bianca cut in, her wardrobe planning complete. "You can't possibly disagree. Holly just has to go to the party. Doesn't she?" That last was said with coy, little girl wistfulness. It reminded Holly that despite Bianca's sophisticated lifestyle, Detloff was much her senior both in age and experience. Her fashion model's bulldozer personality was actually deferring to him: the child bride, pleading for a favor.

"Indeed, I think she should go," Stephen said. "There are only a few malefics at play in her chart tonight." He tucked the calculator back in his pocket.

Holly blinked in astonishment. Had he computed her horoscope so quickly?

His uncertain expression of moments ago vanished. Now his eyes sparkled.

"In fact, I see strong hints of romantic Venusian and Lunar aspects. You really must not dodge this challenge, my dear." Then Stephen added, "But . . . perhaps you're tired or hungry?"

Bianca shut off that escape route. "Oh, she slept for hours in the car, and we had a huge early supper on the road. Come on, Holly. We have to get dressed. And I promise I'll be ready on time, Stephen. Truly!" Her hand closed around Holly's and she towed her sister up the stairs.

Holly followed like a puppet, feeling buffeted by the rush of events. Her sister, especially when in the presence of Stephen Detloff, was all fire and jewel brightness, an irresistible force. She was the embodiment of all those beautiful people Holly had seen on television, and envied for their carefree natures.

The second story of Scorpio House was as strikingly dramatic as its first. The carpeting on the upper level featured a swirling black and white pattern, and the pile was so deep and plush that it made footing deceptive. Furniture and wall décor were equally unusual, like nothing Holly had ever seen.

As Bianca towed her along a hallway, Holly mentally debated pros and cons. She shouldn't let Bianca highjack her like this, so soon after their father's death. And yet . . . it *would* be exciting to plunge into her sister's social circle. The reclusive little caterpillar from Norris Falls might discover she was actually a butterfly! This party was likely to be an interesting gathering of Dark Lake's artists and intelligentsia. She wouldn't have to listen to her father and his cronies reminiscing about old wars. Nor would she need to hide behind household chores.

"Bianca," Holly protested mildly, "I haven't a thing to wear that's suitable for something like this."

"Good God! Don't be silly!" Bianca led the way into an enormous bedroom. The chic, uniformed black woman was laying out clothing on a queen-sized bed. Steam billowed through a connecting door. Holly suspected a bath was being drawn. "Stephen said this room was *you,* but I picked out some of the furnishings and stuff. I hope you like it, Pet." Bianca actually sounded anxious for approval.

Holly gazed around the spacious boudoir. The walls and drapes were a muted yellow, accented with touches of burnt sienna and dark turquoise. Her suitcases stood near a closet, and someone—Melanie?—had placed her African violets on a marble-topped table by a large window.

"He was right," Holly said softly. "I love these colors, this room."

"Isn't that crazy?" Bianca giggled. "We're sisters, and I couldn't begin to imagine your favorite colors. But Stephen knew them to the last detail. Oh, forget those!" Holly had started to open her suitcases. Bianca snatched them from her grasp and tossed them aside like so much trash. "From now on, that bargain basement stuff is out. Tomorrow, we go shopping. The works, Pet. From the skin out. Melanie, will you . . . ooh!" Bianca had looked at her watch. Now she squealed and dashed out of the room without bothering to explain where she was going.

Holly looked uncertainly at Melanie. The maid lifted a dark, expressive eyebrow and shrugged. "Would you like to have your bath now, Miss?" It struck Holly that in Scorpio House even the servants were more composed and sophisticated than Holly Frey, the ultimate rube. With a sigh, she nodded.

She had begun to strip off her clothes when her eyes were drawn to a painting on the wall to her left. A dancer floated against an ethereal, otherworldly background composed of blue-on-blue tones. The figure was lissome, asexual, with huge, luminous yellowish eyes, like those of an impossible cat. That gaze spoke of unfathomable secrets, and the full mouth smiled, amused by the universe.

Melanie noticed Holly's stare and explained, "That's a Graham painting. *Aquarius*, I think Mr. Detloff called it. He ordered that it be hung there. He was quite particular about that."

As Melanie went into the bathroom to complete preparations there, Holly continued to examine the picture, fascinated. Her knowledge of art was limited to the I-know-what-I-like school. And in a peculiar, shivery way, she liked this painting. A "Graham," Melanie said. That must be the Russ Graham Bianca had referred to earlier in the day. He was Stephen Detloff's artist, and presumably *Aquarius* had been rendered as a cover for one of "Scorpio's" numerous and popular books.

Aquarius. Holly's sign.

Stephen Detloff certainly lived his profession, even down to designing the décor in his mansion's guest bedrooms.

Graham's painting was colorfully commercial. Holly could envision its gracing a book jacket, enticing an undecided browser to buy. But there was a great deal more to the picture than salesmanship. The artist hadn't stopped with creating an attractive image; he had included an illusion of watery depths and an enigmatic asexual figure to hint at mystery. Examining the effect, Holly felt she was like the figure—suspended amid tumbling excitement, even peril. Was it all a trick of the eye, or was there really that much to the picture? And what manner of artist could capture so many things at once in lifeless paint?

"Ready, Miss," Melanie called.

Holly allowed herself to be enticed away from the haunting artwork and indulged in the luxury of a long hot bath. Melanie insisted on helping her blow-dry and style her hair. "I wouldn't do anything different with it, Miss," the servant commented. "Maybe clip it a bit here at the back. But it's just the right length. Got a natural wave, too, just like Mrs. Detloff's."

There was new lingerie waiting, and a silken, pale aqua colored dress. Holly knew this must be the "Lauritz" fashion Bianca had mentioned and feared it wouldn't fit; the older Frey sister was several inches taller and ten pounds—at least—thinner. But Melanie had no difficulty hooking the closure. Holly was eyeing the final results in disbelief when Bianca swept back into the room on a cloud of exotic scent.

"I can't wear this," Holly protested. She was much bustier than her sister, and the result was exceedingly décolleté. As she tried to fluff up the fabric over her frontage, she asked, "Haven't you got a pin or scarf or something to—"

Bianca slapped her hands. "Don't hide cleavage like that under a Mother Hubbard. What's the matter with you? This isn't Norris Falls. It looks wonderful. Leave it alone."

Holly was tempted to retort that her sister might well talk. Bianca's russet brocade gown had a halter top which adequately concealed everything but her beautifully tanned shoulders.

Then Holly looked at her reflection again with a shocked sense of re-discovery.

The dress *did* look wonderful. It had been a long time since she'd had the time, or the spirit, to regard herself in a flattering light. And she had never had a personal maid to do lovely things to her hair, let alone money enough for a beautiful dress. Bianca fastened an antique silver and dark amethyst necklace about her sister's throat, whispering, "A present from me to you, Pet. Your birthstone."

Yielding to temptation, Holly smiled and murmured her

thanks. She felt a bit sinful. But surely fate wouldn't begrudge her a *little* pampering. For a long time, she'd thirsted for the heady wine Bianca was drinking, living vicariously in her sister's world of publishing moguls, artists, writers, and the *haute monde.*

Bianca laid her head against her sibling's. Their images peered back at them from the mirror. Bianca's copper-colored hair had been swept up elaborately to one side in a eye-catching coiffure. Holly's "do" was simpler, her hair a bit darker, close to auburn. But all in all, the family resemblance was very apparent. Holly allowed herself to relax a bit, and Bianca exclaimed, "That's it! That all-knowing little smile of yours. Use that and it'll knock 'em dead, believe me."

An uncharitable thought intruded. Holly wondered if she were hearing selfless enthusiasm or simply delight in a "project"—the joy of manipulation that would transform kid sister into a femme fatale.

Before Holly could mull the question at length, Bianca swept a white velour shawl about her sibling's shoulders. "Thanks so much, Melanie," she said with obvious fondness. "You are a true artist, and an absolute gem." Then she was hurrying Holly through the confusing upstairs hallways and down the great staircase.

Stephen was waiting in the foyer. It was plain he was impatient, but his slight frown melted as he saw Bianca. He was again the ultimate sorcerer, clad in a beautifully tailored wine-dark suit with black piping. He only needed a cape to complete the effect.

"Sorry to be late," Bianca said. "But put me in a bubble bath and you know I forget about time, darling . . ."

"Understandable, my watery Cancer, with your proud little self-admiring Aries Moon," Stephen said, winking at

Holly. Then he sobered and asked her, "You aren't troubled by this outing, are you? I wouldn't want to offend your tender conscience."

She assured him she was fine with the arrangements, wishing he hadn't reminded her of lingering uncertainties about the propriety of all this.

Outside, in the half-light of early evening, Holly sank into the plush back seat of Stephen's luxury sedan. As he started the car he turned to smile possessively at Bianca, the wizard doting on his consort.

Detloff's vehicle was whisper quiet. Holly was barely conscious they were moving. She stared out the window, soaking up the sights of her new neighborhood.

The blacktop road curved and twisted, sometimes hugging the shore of Dark Lake, sometimes turning to run hundreds of feet away from the water. Now and then the car's headlights shone on sand dunes or densely wooded sections. It occurred to Holly that she had no idea where they were going. Well, from what Bianca had said, the Martins were also residents of Dark Lake, so surely this trip wouldn't take long.

Stephen and Bianca were discussing a future European tour they hoped to take. Holly listened with half an ear, amused to be eavesdropping on her sister, the globe-trotter.

"My Own," Stephen said in a coaxing manner, "the wait will definitely be worth it. I can promise you a splendid . . . why, what's wrong?"

Bianca shuddered, drawing her fur capelet more closely about her throat. Holly followed her sister's stare. She was looking toward two identical lakeside homes. They were palatial residences, their wide lawns bordered by perfectly trimmed hedges.

"I'm sorry, Stephen. I know it's silly of me. But every time

37

we pass Kyle's home at night I can't help remembering what happened there. It gives me chills."

"I wish you'd never heard about that," the astrologer said, his tone sharp.

"Oh, I would have learned eventually, darling. It's a favorite topic with every local gossip. I don't know why it upsets me so. Why, I never even knew Alanna Preis."

"She was a lovely young woman, though not nearly as lovely as you, My Own." Stephen's voice had softened, and he reached out briefly to stroke Bianca's hair, then returned his hand to the steering wheel. "But she had a terribly occluded Pluto. Nothing like that is in your chart. Please don't let it prey upon you."

"Poor Kyle! And poor Russ!" Bianca added. "I do hope they won't quarrel tonight. After all, it *has* been over a year—"

The car swerved on the narrow road as Stephen jerked the wheel convulsively. Bianca shrieked and he hastily corrected his mistake, then brought the sedan to a bouncing stop.

"You don't mean that they'll both be there?" he demanded. "How could you? What were you and Cynthia thinking of, to invite them both?"

"We knew what we were—" Bianca began hotly.

"Don't you realize that they haven't met socially ever since it happened?" Stephen Detloff was furious. The green glow of the dash lights made his features look satanic.

"A year! A whole year!" Bianca shouted like a fishwife.

Holly shrank back into her seat, grateful that they seemed to have forgotten her presence. This was like an overdone scene in a television drama, where actors were encouraged to throw objects and explode with raging emotions. But it wasn't a play.

The personalities confronting each other in the front seat

were tumultuously real. Holly felt buffeted by the shock waves of their argument.

"You never should have—"

"Good God! They're grown men. Isn't it time they got over this ridiculous nonsense? They both work with you—constantly! Everybody is sick of tippy-toeing around, trying to make sure they never meet face to face. Have you any idea the trouble Toby has, juggling schedules and appointments to—"

"You don't understand," Stephen growled. Brimstone and the weight of augury dripped from every word. It was as if he were privy to secrets too fearful for mere mortals to know. And as if he were sworn to protect that arcane knowledge from non-initiates. "Bianca, it was a mistake."

Holly had never heard such an ominous final pronouncement. Familiar with her sister's temper tantrums, she was totally unprepared for what happened next.

"Did we? Did I? Oh, *Stephen!*" Bianca wailed. "I didn't realize . . . Cynth and I just wanted them to kiss and make up." She was almost sobbing.

"I doubt it will be that simple." Stephen was all wisdom, the voice of doom.

"But . . . but Kyle never speaks of it. And Russ certainly doesn't. We thought—"

"It is a deep matter, My Own. Much, much deeper than you have grasped."

As Bianca seemed about to dissolve in tears, Detloff's attitude altered completely. He put his arms about his distraught wife and drew her close, speaking gently.

"Ah! No, don't fret. There, there. Forgive my anger. Perhaps . . . perhaps the time is right, after all. I will consult my charts. At any rate, now that it's done, we will hope for the best, shan't we?"

"Oh, I'm so sorry!" Bianca cried, sniffling.

The outburst, Stephen's rage, Bianca's collapse, and the tearful reconciliation had taken place in scant moments. Yet Holly felt as though she'd witnessed a cataclysm, so intense were the feelings involved. What would have happened if love hadn't channeled their passions? She hoped things never came to that.

While Bianca dabbed at her eyes, Stephen put the car in motion again. She glanced at him anxiously and said, "Darling?"

"It was a mistake. Never do that again without consulting me, My Own."

Bianca nodded meekly. Her behavior stunned Holly. This was a complete contrast to her sister's typically super-confident nature.

Stephen sighed heavily and said, "To be perfectly frank, I would relish an ending of their feud. It's been very awkward for me, because I'm, so to speak, the man in the middle. But you can't just shove the two of them into each other's arms. They'll have to do their own hatchet burying."

Detloff turned into a luminaria-flanked driveway leading to a Tudor-style ranch house. Festive lanterns decorated the long, screened porch. Laughter and music spilled from open windows and across the broad lawn. A clutter of cars sat in a paved turn-around at the head of the drive. Stephen eased the sedan into one of the few remaining parking spaces.

Before they stepped out, he said, "My Own, remember: Do not mention Alanna Preis. If Kyle or Russ should bring up the subject, that's their choice, not ours."

"Of course, dearest," Bianca replied, hurt. "I'm not *that* insensitive."

"No, certainly not. But it's easy to forget such things in the middle of a gay party, my love. Especially for someone who wasn't a Dark Lake resident when it happened. The scars run exceedingly deep. Just be careful. We mustn't remind a man that his wife may have had a lover—a lover who was, however briefly, suspected of murdering that wife in a most terrible and brutal fashion."

Chapter 3

Holly felt as though a lump of ice had filled her stomach. So *that* was it! The truth behind Bianca's cryptic comments *en route* to Dark Lake. She'd hinted at some sort of nasty gossip about Russ Graham, but refused to elaborate. Now that she had learned this, Holly almost wished she were back in Norris Falls.

Too late! Stephen was handing the women out of the sedan and escorting them to the house. A pretty young matron with long dark hair waited in the doorway, beckoning to the trio. "Come in, come in! I was beginning to worry you wouldn't make it. But I see you got back from Europe just in time, Stephen."

He pressed her hands and greeted her affectionately. Bianca joined in with compliments on the tall woman's chic red gown. The spacious room just beyond the entry was full of people all talking at once. Soft strains of music served as an undercurrent for conversation.

Bianca slid an arm through her sister's. "Holly, this is Cynthia Martin, my dearest chum. And the most brilliant scholar you'll ever meet. She was presenting a paper at the university when I did that fashion shoot there last year. You remember, surely? I told you about it." Holly nodded dumbly and plastered on a wan smile. Her hostess's eyes twinkled in amused sympathy as Bianca babbled on. "If it hadn't been for her, I'd never have met Stephen and . . . well, that's where it all started!"

"We're so glad you could come, Holly," Cynthia said warmly.

"Well, old man, are you ready to explain—again—why the precession of the equinoxes should be ignored?" An exceedingly tall, slender man had joined the group by the door while Holly had been preoccupied. His bantering tone was aimed at Stephen.

The astrologer made introductions and Holly learned this was Jason Martin, Cynthia's husband. He greeted the newcomer politely, then returned his attention to Stephen. It was obvious the two were resuming an amiable, long-standing debate—scientific skepticism versus the occult.

"Penny! Anne! Rusty!" Bianca exclaimed, sailing into the crowd.

Cynthia shook her head at Bianca's precipitous departure and smiled at Holly.

"Could I take your wrap? I'll collect hers later." She led the way to a walk-in closet. As she hung up the shawl she asked, "Is there anyone here you'd particularly like to meet? Would you care for something to drink? Hard or soft? How about a snack?"

Holly began to unwind. Cynthia would probably make even Attila feel right at home. "A soft drink would be nice, thank you."

"Hey, Cynth! Your table of gobbleables out on the terrace is just about empty. That's a ravenous bunch out there."

"Oh, my!" the hostess said, dismayed to be found lax in feeding her guests. "I'll see to that at once. Holly, this is Maud Rutherford, our resident Den Mother." Cynthia hastily explained Holly's relationship to the Detloffs and finished, "I guarantee she'll be happy to take you under her wing. Sorry to rush. Must feed the hungry lions . . ."

Maud was a plump woman with a jolly face under a cap of cropped grey hair. The title "Den Mother" fit her well. The last of Holly's uneasiness faded as Maud put a generous arm around her shoulders and steered her into the main room. "Stick with me, kid, and you'll be wearing diamonds, or pretzels. Hi, Tuck, Kay . . ."

Introductions flowed. Holly met a number of the famous and near-famous. Dark Lake indeed was a celebrity haven. And to her surprise there was no apparent social uniform. She'd expected a see a bunch of fashion plates, and some people *were* elegantly, handsomely, and expensively dressed. Others, though, wore what she could only think of as "summer resort casual." A further surprise was that there was no obvious age, gender, or class gap. Everyone mingled freely. The noise level, aside from the muted background music, was a laughter-broken hum.

"Here, let's sneak along the wall, so they can't find us," Maud said, *sotto voce*.

Holly grinned at the hammy, conspiratorial words, following Maud's bright pink flowered caftan to an unoccupied sofa in a side room. "Do we *want* to avoid capture?" Holly said, playing the game.

Maud plopped down onto the couch with a relieved sigh, and Holly sat beside her. "Nope, but my feet can't take all that standing around, honey," the older woman replied. "Let the mountain come to mama, right?"

"Right!" Holly appreciated the respite. She was more than content to stand—or sit—back and observe the social waters further before taking a deeper plunge. And Maud seemed like a very good lifeguard for such a plan.

At that moment, a servant came up and offered her a glass brimming with ice and cola. She accepted with much thanks. Maud nodded and said, "How about fetching another Collins for me, Jessup, and a sandwich? A real one, not one of those mouse munchies the hordes are devouring. I'm starving!"

The servant's mouth twitched, but he nodded and hurried off to execute her order.

"He seems to know you pretty well," Holly ventured.

Maud fanned herself with a cocktail napkin and a chuckle heaved her ample bosom. Like Old Saint Nick, when she laughed, she laughed all over, and made the onlooker want to join in. "Honey, everybody knows me. It's the penalty of inheriting scads of money and having no occupation but dabbling in other people's affairs. Finger in every pie. Ha! Maybe that's why they're so pudgy, huh?" She wiggled her be-ringed digits. Suddenly, in a confidential tone, she pressed Holly's arm and said, "See the Amazon wearing electric blue over there? Kay Butler, the entertainer. She's with a touring company in Chicago, right now. And that distinguished looking guy with the beard? Hevelin, the anthropologist . . ."

As she went on, Holly appreciated that Maud was giving her a guided tour of the cream of the Dark Lake community. Trying to keep track of the flood of names, Holly noticed that Stephen glanced in her direction now and then. He was still deep in discussion with Jason, but the astrologer was also surreptitiously keeping an eye on her. Once, his gaze shifted toward Maud, and a reassured smile creased his saturnine face. It was nice to know her brother-in-law cared enough to check on whether or not she was in good hands—and plainly he'd decided she was. Holly agreed.

"Tucker, the writer, and Lavell—hotel chains," Maud's running commentary continued.

Hairs prickled on the back of Holly's neck, warning her that she was under scrutiny. Hastily, she scanned the area and saw a man sitting near the window at the far end of the room. He was alone, barely visible between milling party-goers, and looking intently at the newcomer.

At first Holly wondered if she was mistaken. Perhaps he was merely gazing blankly into nothing, as people often did when lost in thought.

No. His focus was most definitely on her. And it was a disturbingly intense stare, like a laser.

She became conscious of her dress's low neckline. Was the man ogling her lustfully? Doubtful. That wasn't a leer. It was a very different sort of look, and quite unsettling. Despite that, she made an effort to pull the fabric of the gown up.

". . . and Betty Johnson had better quit showing so much skin, or she's gonna end up like poor Alanna Preis," Maud was saying.

Suddenly forgetting the laser-eyed stranger, Holly gulped and said, "Alanna Preis? What about her?"

"Bianca didn't tell you? That's awful. You oughta be forewarned, kid. A girl has to be on her guard."

"Against what?" That lump of ice was back in Holly's belly, and much, much colder than it had been before.

"Surely . . . didn't they cover it on the news? Well, maybe not out of state. I forgot that you're new to Dark Lake. The Butcher Knife Murderer, the police call him," Maud explained with a shiver. "He's killed at least six women, so far. Poor Alanna wasn't the last one either. As I recall, there was another case up in Gary a few weeks ago."

Holly sat very still, stunned. She'd been rattled by the earlier revelation about Alanna Preis's murder. But it seemed that ghastly crime wasn't an isolated incident. A serial killer! One who was, by Maud's account, still at large.

"Murdered right there in her own home, poor thing," Maud said, shaking her head sadly. "Still gives me nightmares to think about it. Alanna and Kyle live . . . lived . . .

46

right down the road from me. And now . . . no way of telling when that monster will strike again. According to the police, we're overdue for another killing, so lock your door, sweetie."

"The . . . the police," Holly stammered, "must have some clues—"

"Not a hint. I've got a friend on the force, and he admits it's got 'em baffled. No rhyme or reason to his . . . targets, they say. Can you imagine? They even questioned Kyle about it. His secretary kept telling them he was in his Chicago office all evening. And that place is like a fortress. I heard the cops even checked the date stamps and timers in the company parking garage to see if Kyle really was there. Of course he was! The nerve of them! Suspecting for a moment that he could have been guilty of her murder! With his beautiful wife dead like that! And I thought they were *never* going to quit hounding Russ . . ." Maud's words carried a mixture of horrified revulsion and that all-too-human fascination with violence lurking even in some gentler members of the species.

"I . . . I do believe I may have read something in the newspaper about the incident," Holly said, "now that you mention it."

"Just nothing for the police to trace," Maud went on in a low, confiding tone. "I gather he uses a discount store butcher knife, and doesn't leave any fingerprints. That fiend could be anywhere. And he has to be crazy. His victim is always a woman, stabbed dozens of times, like he couldn't stop himself. All of us shake in our boots whenever we think about it, wondering who's next . . ."

Holly's throat was tight, a tinge of nausea bubbling just behind her breastbone. And her nerves weren't helped in the slightest by that man across the room staring holes through her.

Murder most foul and brutal, and aimed solely at women!

Yes, she *did* remember the news accounts now. It had all seemed so remote, back in Norris Falls. Nothing that would ever affect *her*.

But now she was residing in the very heart of the place where it was happening. Not a mile from where one of the murderer's victims had died.

"Alanna was such a charming, lovely little thing, and sweet as an angel," Maud said, wiping away a tear. "We never dreamed a horrible thing like that could happen to any of us. And it looked so bad for Russ for a while, what with Kyle off in the city, and Russ finding her body. I never had any doubts at all about Russ, not for a second! Why, with his background, if he committed murder, you can bet your bottom dollar he'd *shoot* whoever he was after, not stab 'em. But it sure was awfully sticky for him there for a while, after . . . well, after what had gone on."

"What had gone on?" Holly wondered aloud, recalling Bianca's veiled comments and Stephen's remark in the car. Had Russ Graham been Alanna's lover?

"Well, you know . . . why, Kyle!" Maud elided smoothly into an effusive, overly cheery greeting. The handsome blond man Holly had met that afternoon stood before them. Maud heaved herself to her feet and planted a noisy, smacking kiss on his lips as he hugged her fondly. "Now where have you been hiding yourself?" she demanded in mock anger.

"Mother had to put a magazine to bed. Caused a bit of a delay," Kyle Preis explained absently. Most of his attention was fixed on Holly. "Miss Frey, isn't it? We met earlier today, but much too briefly. I was afraid you wouldn't be here when I heard . . . I was so sorry about your father. I'm glad you did decide to come. Maybe we can help you forget your sorrow for a while."

"Thank you," Holly murmured. Somehow, she found her

hands clasped in his and she smiled up at him warily. Kyle oozed charm, but there was inner tension in his grip, a symptom she could hardly fail to recognize after all those months caring for her late father.

"Oh, ho ho!" Maud said archly, laughing. "Fast work, buddy boy! You watch out for him, honey. Biggest heart-breaker in these parts."

"How you lie, Maud, baby," Kyle retorted, his eyes remaining on her companion.

Holly reminded herself he was a widower, and that he, too, had suffered the loss of someone very close to him. For some reason, the thought increased her wariness. This man was undeniably attractive, and, as most women would, she enjoyed his flattery and his strong, masculine presence. And yet . . .

"Did you bring your recording gear tonight?" Maud said, poking Kyle in the ribs and winking at Holly. "Gotta watch him close. He's a real sneak. He hid some mikes at one of our parties and scrambled up all the voices on the playback. It was positively embarrassing, but funny as hell. You ought to join the CIA, Kyle, and teach the spy guys some tricks."

"Cut it out," he muttered, perching on the arm of the sofa, his hand continuing to hold Holly's. "You'll scare her off, and we don't want that, do we? Here I was looking forward to cornering her every time I have to drop in on Stephen . . ."

At his level of income and power, Preis surely dated many women, a lot of them famous and movie star gorgeous. Compliments and talk about cornering her were simply part of his game, pleasant to listen to, but hardly anything to be taken seriously. "I hope we'll meet again in the future, yes," Holly said coyly, playing her part in the exchange.

He pounced on her response. "I'm counting on it. I think you'll find that—"

"Did you ever hear of anything so idiotic?" a strident female voice shrilled above the crowd's hum. There was an answering burst of raucous guffaws. Kyle's hand spasmed almost painfully around Holly's, and a muscle tightened along his jawline.

With barely disguised distaste, Maud said, "I didn't know Sylvia was coming tonight."

"Yes, she's here," Kyle said, very curt. Then his manner shifted again, becoming suave and relaxed. He let go of Holly's hand and rose, turning toward the center of the main room, where a group of partygoers surrounded an older woman.

Sylvia. Holly mulled the name. That must be Sylvia Preis, Kyle's mother.

Bianca had described her as a fabulously wealthy widow who owned the publishing empire in partnership with her son. Both of them had been featured prominently in national news magazines and television productions. When Bianca spoke of Sylvia, she'd sounded disapproving, to say the least. Watching the performance in the adjacent room, Holly now understood why.

"Kyle! Heart o' my heart, come here and tell the people how we screwed Beatley but good, baby," Sylvia ordered the young man. Sycophants surrounding her cheered admiringly. Other guests, though, rolled their eyes, and some sneered.

Holly expected Kyle to show reluctance to obey, given his reaction to hearing Sylvia's voice. But he didn't hesitate. By the time he reached his mother's side he was grinning widely and nodding as she said, "Baby, we are gonna eat up ole Mays Beatley, ain't we?"

For a split second, Sylvia looked over at Holly. There was unmasked malevolence in the woman's eyes. The visual encounter hurled Holly back to Norris Falls, to far too many oc-

casions when she'd had to deal with one of her father's rages.
Then Sylvia's attention jerked away as the publisher launched
into a graphic, obscenity-riddled description of the absent
Beatley, to the cackling enjoyment of her fawning audience.

Simultaneously intrigued and appalled, Holly couldn't re-
sist studying Kyle's mother, almost as though she were seeing
a laboratory specimen. Sylvia's hair was brittle-dry bleached
platinum blonde. She had the firm, curvy body of starlet,
probably assisted by considerable surgery. That tucked and
rearranged package was encased in a skin-tight black leather
dress which made the fifty-plus publishing mogul look like a
cheap hooker. It was very plain that she was braless, but those
breasts had been enhanced with silicone, belying their
owner's age. The effect Sylvia tried to achieve was spoiled by
a face which couldn't defeat time and by an indulgent lifestyle. Her features were hard, jaded, and layered with thick
makeup, a road map of her ruthless scramble for success. She
practically hung on her son's arm and lapped up her toadies'
flattery. In every way, Sylvia Preis was the sort of woman
most other women hated on sight.

Cynthia came into the side room, cutting off Holly's view
of the disgusting scene around Sylvia. "There you are! I've
been looking for you. Are you at all interested in good prints?
Jason and I have picked up some really nice ones recently. I'd
be happy to show them to you."

"Go right ahead, honey," Maud said, waving enthusiasti-
cally to someone approaching from another room. It was obvious she wouldn't be alone for long.

Holly recalled Bianca's advice to admire her hosts' prints,
but by now she didn't really need that incentive. Cynthia and
Jason had impressed her as well educated, cultured people,
and she was eager to see what beautiful objects they might
have selected to decorate their home. Holly rose and followed

51

Mrs. Martin through the crowd, Cynthia pausing now and then to exchange quick little comments with her other guests.

Suddenly she stopped and said, "Russ, you haven't seen our latest acquisitions, either, have you?"

Holly tensed, apprehensive. They were standing before the man who'd been staring at her earlier.

Russ. Of course. Russ Graham. The man who had created the *Aquarius* painting hanging in her bedroom. And the man who had discovered the body of Alanna Preis, Kyle's murdered wife. The man who had been suspected, at least briefly, of that murder.

And Maud and Stephen had hinted that Russ might have been Alanna's lover as well.

The artist got to his feet. He was taller and leaner than Kyle Preis, and his hair was dark, a bit long, and wavy. Graham was simply and neatly dressed in a plain white shirt and black cord slacks; he didn't much resemble the traditional image of a devil-may-care artist. Holly could see, at this close range, that those piercing eyes were an odd, pale shade of blue. That unnerving gaze was locked on her right now, although he was speaking to Cynthia. "No, I haven't. New stuff? Are you getting up a tour?"

Holly was almost startled to find that he had a pleasant, calm baritone voice. She'd expected something more dramatic, in keeping with his profession, and that stare.

"Not yet. Just Holly and you. Oh, you haven't met Holly, have you? Holly Frey, this is Russ Graham. Russ, Holly is Bianca's sister." Cynthia turned to Holly and added, "Russ is one of our resident artists here at Dark Lake—"

"Commercial artist," he corrected her. Did Holly detect a tinge of bitterness in the words? Graham made no effort to shake her hand, and she was too ill at ease to initiate the gesture.

52

After an awkward pause, their hostess said with forced brightness, "The prints are this way, people." Keenly aware that the man with the burning eyes was right behind her, Holly followed Cynthia to a quieter part of the Martins' home. Their artwork was housed in a miniature gallery, a room nearly bare of furniture. The walls were covered with framed artwork and glass cases displayed sculptures.

Interested, but feeling quite ignorant, Holly listened closely as Cynthia described the treasures. Some prints were small. Others occupied several square feet. Subject matter ranged from sophisticated cartoons to powerful realism and surrealism to totally non-representational material.

"This is another of those anatomical studies, isn't it?" Russ Graham remarked, pointing to a venous study in reds, pinks, and faded blues.

Cynthia nodded. "Mother and Dad picked it up in Vienna at a medical conference. My parents are doctors," she added, by way of explanation to Holly. "They began collecting such things as a joke, bringing back blowups of elaborately printed etchings of human organs, and then . . ."

"It got out of hand," Russ finished with a wry smile.

"I . . . I like this one," Holly said timidly, afraid of exposing her lack of knowledge.

She indicated a microscopically detailed red leaf lying on a greyish-blue background. The leaf's veins were incredibly delicate wisps of botanic fragility.

"You have good taste." Graham's tone was flat, the compliment unvarnished.

Holly wasn't sure if she felt triumphant or irritated. This aloof, taciturn man had approved her judgment. Shouldn't she be pleased that an artist had found her choice acceptable? Instead, she wanted, perversely, to find some criticism of the print she had just admired.

He spared her the trouble of deciding what to do by walking over to another wall and examining the large print hanging there. "This is new, Cynth."

"Oh, yes. A real find. We got it at auction. That's *Romaunt of the Rose*."

Holly eyed the work with a frown. The "rose" of the title was quite apparent. It was wistfully stranded on a cream-colored field. But she could see no romance in the ochre *thing*, an elongated abomination crawling toward the flower. The painting seemed a blatant *double entendre*.

She was about to comment to that effect when Russ Graham threw back his head and laughed, a hearty, un-restrained bellow. "That, Cynth, is the most obscene thing I've seen in weeks."

Their hostess chuckled and blushed slightly. "It is, isn't it? But intriguing . . ."

"Hey, everybody! All aboard for Pietro's!" It was Maud, hailing them from the gallery's doorway. "Wondered where you'ns had got to. Come on, or they'll run out of mushroom lasagna before I get there!"

"Oh, dear! I just knew this would happen. It always does," Cynthia said, and led the way back to the main party. She didn't appear distressed, merely anxious to make sure that the excursion went smoothly.

The main room was pandemonium, with people already banging out the door.

Stephen stood in the foyer, craning his neck, looking about worriedly, searchingly.

Bianca fussed at him, urging him to hurry. Holly was struck by their differing attitudes toward her: Stephen concerned, Bianca oblivious to her sister's whereabouts or desires, but . . . that was nothing new.

"Maud's right," Russ Graham said. "This sort of stampede will clean out Pietro's kitchen in no time, *and* fatten his cash register. Do you like Italian food, Miss Frey?"

Holly opened her mouth to reply, then was startled to silence as someone hurrying out bumped into her.

"Oh, good. Can she ride with you, Russ?" Cynthia was asking. "It would be so much simpler than trying to work our way over to Stephen and Bianca."

"All right with me," the artist said with a shrug. He spoke loudly to make himself heard over the exiting crowd. "I can't move my car anyway until some of this thundering herd gets out of the drive."

All about Holly, people were shouting and laughing, promising to meet one another at the restaurant, issuing dares to see who would arrive first. Cynthia was signaling to Stephen across the crowd, pantomiming for him the arrangements for his sister-in-law's transportation. The astrologer intercepted that silent communication and nodded. Then he and Bianca were swallowed up in the stream flowing outdoors.

Holly choked down an urge to run after them. Bianca had said she was launching her sister into the social waters of Dark Lake. But Holly felt like she was a non-swimmer being thrown in at the nine-foot level. She cast a sidelong glance at the man beside her—the man with the laser stare and curt manner, the man who refused to shake her hand.

Most of all, remembering that Alanna Preis had been murdered, and that Russ Graham had found her body.

Why hadn't Cynthia arranged for her to ride with Kyle instead of this brooding stranger?

Then Holly heard Sylvia Preis's distinctive bray. The swarm of toadies engulfed her and her son. Kyle peered back over his shoulder. His gaze fell on Holly and Russ Graham, and Preis's handsome face tightened.

Sylvia, too, spared them a look. Her eyes narrowed in anger. In the next instant, she and Kyle and their corona of admirers were through the foyer and out of sight.

"Here's your stole, Holly," Cynthia said. She waved cheerily to the last of the departing party goers. "Jason and I will tidy up a bit and follow. See you at Pietro's."

Russ Graham took the stole from her and draped it about Holly's bare arms. "We'd better get started, Miss Frey."

Moving in a fog, Holly let him lead her to his car. It was a well-worn Cherokee, the back end filled with artist's paraphernalia and assorted junk. His face unreadable, he handed her into the vehicle, carefully making certain the hem of her skirt wouldn't be mangled when he closed the door.

When that door slammed, Holly jumped. She sat up very straight, braced for anything as Graham got behind the wheel and started the engine.

He drove out onto the blacktop road and began paralleling the lake, heading west. Holly was mildly surprised to learn that Graham was no hot-rodder. He drove within posted limits and kept strictly to his side of the road. There was nothing in his behavior to alarm her.

And yet a litany ran through her brain again and again, haunting phrases recently heard: *The Butcher Knife Murderer. Alanna Preis. The victim is always a woman. Russ Graham found her body.*

There was also that maddeningly cryptic warning from Bianca and Stephen: *It would be better if you were safely at Scorpio House when . . .*

But she wasn't at Scorpio House. She was sitting beside the man with the fiery eyes. All around her lay the mysterious black, northern Indiana night. Holly was alone with a man she'd met only minutes ago, and going she knew not where.

"Not much of a talker, are you?" Graham asked.

He had turned off the Dark Lake road onto a state highway. On either side now shone neon lights of gas stations and eateries. Their eerie gleam illuminated Graham's lean face. When he'd spoken, he'd glanced briefly at Holly, then quickly returned his attention to the road. His obvious safety consciousness reassured her a bit.

She forced herself to say lightly, "I might say the same for you. But I suppose 'artistic temperament' gives you a handy excuse."

"Does it?" Graham snorted, a kind of half laugh. "Is that a polite way of telling me I'm anti-social? I'm not, at least not dedicated about it. But for reasons we won't discuss, I haven't been much of a partygoer for quite a while."

For quite a while. Since Alanna Preis's murder?

The Cherokee ate up miles, pavement flowing back beneath the headlights.

A forest of sodium-barium lamps rose ahead, casting their glow over a superhighway entrance ramp. Graham merged smoothly with the traffic flow on I-94.

Holly wondered where they were going. She had no idea where Pietro's was.

Gary? East Chicago? Hammond? In fact, there was no way to be sure Graham was even heading for the place where the rest of the party had gone.

"You planning to stay long at Dark Lake?"

She dragged herself out of nervous musing. "I . . . I'm not . . . oh, probably. Things are still up in the air." A silence was the only response to her babbling. Holly let it go on as long as she could stand, then asked, "Do you live far from Scorpio House?"

"About half a mile."

The information both interested and alarmed her. Holly's

reactions to Graham had become ambiguous. His solemn manner tempted her to tickle him, to see if she could make him laugh as wholeheartedly as he had in the gallery. But . . . there were all those rumors, and his grim past, intertwined with Alanna Preis's murder. Holly felt edgy, and at the same time drawn in by the artist's unassuming manner. She speculated on what his personality was like when terrible clouds of suspicion didn't hang over him.

"I used to keep the studio just for summer use," he said. "But I finally figured out that it was cheaper to live here year-round, even counting transportation in and out of Chi. Unlike Maud, and a few others I could name, I didn't inherit wealth. I have to scratch to keep even." Holly said nothing, watching him thoughtfully. He darted a look toward her, then concentrated on the road. Graham seemed as uneasy under her scrutiny as she was under his. "Bianca says you were taking care of your father."

"Yes. He died a couple of weeks ago."

Instead of the formal condolences Holly expected, he said, "She mentioned a lingering illness. That must have been a real ball to deal with. Were you close?"

Startled into frankness, Holly blurted, "No, not toward the end. He'd become very . . . difficult, a stranger, in a sense. Occasionally demented and violent, though fortunately he was too weak by then to be much of a threat to anyone but himself."

"In pain?" Again, Graham's question was terse, cut to the bone.

"The doctors said not. Probably, by that stage of the disease, Father didn't realize what was happening to him, most of the time. At least, I hope not. He'd . . . given up, in a way. Living in dreams, or maybe nightmares."

"Rough. But a better death than some people have." The

artist's voice was bitter. Was he thinking of Alanna, ripped by a murderer's knife? "Demented. That sounds particularly ugly."

"It was. Caused by an obscure disease no one's ever heard of."

"Oh?" Graham's tone was skeptical. One dark eyebrow lifted.

"Yes. Progressive lenticular degeneration," Holly pronounced. She'd spent a lot of time memorizing the term and listening to doctors expound upon it. "No cure for it, or, as the doctors put it, 'There is no specific treatment.' "

"Bianca said as much, but I take everything she says with salt," Graham muttered. No apology for his doubt. Just acceptance of the facts. "But I gather she was paying the bills."

"I'll give her that. Even if she seconded his refusal to go into a hospice," Holly said. With difficulty, she mastered her urge to bitch. It wouldn't do any good now, any more than it had at the time.

"Good thing you were there. Good for him, I mean. Bianca doesn't strike me as the type to nurse the terminally ill. As a matter of fact, neither do you."

"I'm tougher than I look," Holly flared. She added with dripping sarcasm, "You should see my lamp and my stained and tattered Victorian nurse's uniform . . ."

Suddenly, her heart was in her throat.

Ahead of them, appallingly close, a confused driver had stalled his vehicle crossways in traffic, completely blocking their lane. Behind and around them, cars and trucks roared.

There was no space—or time!—to cut left to dodge the other car. No break in a 70-mph river of metal and rubber.

Everything around Holly seemed to shift into slow motion. She had an odd sense that she was simultaneously a spectator, rigid with fright, and watching herself and what was happening with clinical detachment.

This was crazy! Unfair!

She had barely started her new life, and now it was all going to end in a gory, bone-shattering auto crash. What a cruel jest of fate!

Russ Graham was cursing and stomping on the brakes and twisting the steering wheel hard. The car careened to the right. Slithering and fish-tailing, the Cherokee plowed along the graveled berm. Hemmed between the stalled car and the guardrail, Graham skillfully manhandled his vehicle through the narrow opening.

"Stupid bastard!" he spat, as he swerved back onto the expressway lane.

"What . . . what did he think he was doing?"

"Who the hell knows?" The artist let his fury pour out in a stream of obscenities. Then he cooled down a bit and said, "One of these brain-dead morons who missed his exit. He was probably trying to back up and get to it."

"But he'll be killed!" Holly twisted in the seat, peering out the back window.

The Cherokee had topped a rise, though, and whatever tragedy might be taking place back at the scene of their near accident now was cut off from view.

"Serve him right," Graham snapped. "So long as he doesn't take anyone else with him."

"Didn't you ever make a mistake? Maybe that's what happened to him."

"Yeah, I've made mistakes. Plenty. But not where they really counted, and not where they could get other people killed!"

The smothered rage in his words appalled her. Then Holly

realized his outburst was more than likely due to adrenaline overload. Only his incredibly quick reflexes had saved them. Wasn't the man entitled to exhibit anger and verbal release? Her stomach was doing flip-flops. Graham's must be in turmoil.

"I . . . uh . . . I shouldn't have yelled at you," he said, barely audible. After a few moments, he abruptly changed the subject. "Have you met Toby yet?"

"Y . . . yes. He seems very nice, very helpful."

They were exiting I-94. Graham didn't speak again until the Cherokee was rolling along a feeder road. Then he said, "I'd appreciate it if you'd give Toby a message next time you see him. Tell him I've got a visitor I'd like him to meet. Could you do that?"

"Of . . . of course."

"Come along yourself, if you'd like. It's not much of a walk, and the scenery's great."

Holly mulled over the left-handed invitation. Was it an afterthought, or genuine?

And why, if Graham wished to speak to Toby Carmichael, didn't he just phone Scorpio House? Was there an ulterior motive in his request that she relay the message?

Though tempted to voice her questions, she kept mum while Graham drove through the outer suburbs of a city. Brightly lit shopping centers and trade marts bracketed the streets. A few minutes further driving brought them to a sprawling, tile-roofed restaurant. Its rooftop sign winked, "Pietro's." Graham found an empty parking spot, one of the few left.

"Guess we're the last to get here, except for Cynth and Jason," Graham said.

Inside, they found the restaurant a-hum with many of the same people who'd been at the Martins' party. A red-cheeked, rotund man in a chef's cap and apron greeted the new arrivals. "Ah, my friend Russ! What would you like?"

Graham consulted Holly, asking, "Pizza? Any problems?"

"No anchovies."

His face split in a delighted grin. "Me too. Loathe the things. A big one, Pietro, but no fish. Eh?" The proprietor grinned and bellowed instructions to his staff behind the counter.

"Over there," Graham said, taking Holly's elbow. "I see a free booth, wonders to behold." He forced a path through enthusiastic dancers, shielding her from buffets. She was struck by the contrast in his manner—gallantry and surliness.

Bianca, Stephen, and half a dozen other partiers sat at a nearby table. Holly's sister didn't even look up from her spirited conversation, but Stephen noticed the new arrivals and waved a greeting. Holly wondered if it was only her imagination that she read an easing of anxiety in the astrologer's expression. Had he been worried? Seeing more "malefics" in her horoscope? Did "malefics" include an almost fatal collision?

Russ Graham handed her into the booth and slid into the opposite seat. Once again, his pale eyes bored holes through her. Was such an intent stare natural for him?

She wanted to challenge him on the point, but chose not to, for the present. He *had* saved her life with his skillful driving.

Nevertheless, she was relieved when he turned his attention to the crowd.

"You know, these people could afford to go to a restaurant with five times the prices and twenty times the carte available at Pietro's. But this is currently Dark Lake's 'in' place to eat. They think of it as 'intimate.' I'm sure they'd—"

"Hello, Holly . . . Russ." The voice was so soft she almost didn't hear it amid the music and loud conversations.

Kyle Preis stood beside the booth.

Gooseflesh prickled Holly's arms. Here was the man whose wife had been brutally murdered, confronting the man who had found her body.

The man who also was Alanna Preis's lover?

According to Stephen, these two hadn't met for a year. And the birth of their estrangement had been bloody and violent death.

Now they were face to face, and Holly was the reluctant witness of whatever was going to happen.

Chapter 4

"Mind if I sit down?" Kyle asked, quite deferential.

Holly tried to gauge Russ's expression, and failed. He might have been playing it cool or doing an excellent job of smothering hate. After a long hesitation he nodded. Kyle dragged an empty chair up and placed it at the end of the booth. As he sat down he rubbed a hand over his chin, apparently weighing what he intended to say.

Beyond his shoulder Holly could see Sylvia in the midst of her yes-people. The publisher was halfway across the crowded restaurant, but her strident laughter was painfully audible. Laughter—but she was looking daggers in Holly's direction.

"It's been a while," Kyle began. He leaned back in his chair and waited for Russ Graham's response.

The two reminded Holly of virile, dangerous male animals carefully circling each other. She'd met both of them only today and couldn't begin to guess at their inner emotions at this moment. How should she interpret Kyle's half frown or Russ's narrowed eyes?

"A while, yes," the artist finally said with quiet understatement.

Holly held her breath, afraid of upsetting this momentary truce between them.

"I figured it was about time we broke the ice. Maybe we should thank Cynth and Bianca for sending us both invitations, don't you think?" Kyle's suggestion carried no hint of sarcasm. He sounded completely sincere. Perhaps he indeed wanted to bury the hatchet.

Holly could have kicked herself for thinking of that phrase. It led inexorably to another thought—an image of a faceless, menacing figure raising a bladed weapon, looming over a helpless woman, soon to be a victim.

Russ studied the publisher minutely, as if trying to read the other man's soul.

"I want you to know," Kyle went on, "that I never swallowed those damned rumors. Not for a second." He was leaning forward, his square face taut with anxiety.

When a server came up to the table he flinched in surprise, then sat back, allowing the woman to lay out dishes, water glasses, and an immense wheel of pizza.

Graham, too, held his peace until the server had left. Then he said with bitter amusement, "Rumors? There were rumors?"

"Oh, hell! Don't pour salt in the wounds, Russ. You know damned well what I'm talking about. I've wrestled tigers trying to push aside all that dirt people kept throwing my way, to cope with what . . . what happened. It's not a thing you can get over in a week or two, or months, come to that."

"No, you can't," the artist agreed, a heavy undercurrent in his words. Was he remembering Alanna? Had he truly loved her? "Yes," he said bleakly, nodding, "it takes quite a while."

"A year?" Kyle prodded, gently, tactfully. Russ regarded him like a lion peering out from the security of a cave. The publisher slammed a fist into his palm. "Dammit, this has gone on long enough. It's ridiculous! You and I ducking around corners to avoid each other—"

"*I* haven't ducked around any corners."

"Hell, you know what I mean. We both work with Stephen, and it's been like juggling dynamite, for us, for Toby, setting up appointments, the whole thing. Look, can't we start fresh?" Kyle's hand went out, open and welcoming. His face was damp with sweat, golden strands of hair sticking to his high forehead. Obviously, this was difficult for him. He wouldn't have been human if he hadn't harbored doubts about Graham, after hearing such rumors. Now he was being generous, overcoming past suspicions and offering to shake hands with a man who might well have been his dead wife's lover.

Russ looked at the outstretched hand for a long moment, then shrugged and took it. It wasn't a firm handshake, Holly could see. But Kyle sighed in relief, as if a burden had dropped from his shoulders. "Thanks, man! It's taken me forever to work up the courage to approach you, you know." Graham's expression was guarded. Before he could say anything, Kyle rushed on, "Listen, I'm throwing a picnic and swim party on the fourth. Can you make it, Russ? I want you there."

"Won't Sylvia have something to say about who gets invitations?"

"No!" Kyle's tone was sharp. "No, this is *my* bash, not hers."

His vehemence had taken Holly aback. Then, with sudden empathy, she understood what was eating him. Filial devotion at war with frustrated desire to be free. No one could mistake Sylvia's behavior for anything but harpy-like possessiveness. She was a textbook example of the tyrannical parent refusing to let go of her nestling. Holly recognized the problem from extensive courses she'd taken while trying to understand her father's illness. His selfishness and unreasonableness weren't his fault, but the effects were very much the same. Only death had at last freed her from filial obligation. Was her longing to lead her own life henceforth so different from Kyle's?

"All right," Russ said simply. "I'll come."

A pleased grin lit up Kyle's face. He offered his hand again, and this time the artist took it without hesitation, though he showed no enthusiasm for what he'd just agreed to.

Immediately, Kyle turned to Holly. "You're a gem to put up with all this nonsense. I hope you know that I want you to come to the party, too. In fact," and his hazel eyes sparkled with mischief, "about now Russ is suspecting that I manufactured this entire encounter just so I could get in a bid for you. Aren't you, Russ? How about it, pretty lady? Please? I've checked it with your chaperone, and she says it's okay."

Chaperone. Holly assumed he meant Bianca. Bianca, the self-centered big sister who'd insisted she yank up all her roots and move to Dark Lake, then instantly abandoned her in deep waters. Holly barely kept from laughing derisively at the term "chaperone."

Kyle was rushing on, eager to convince her. "Stephen won't object, either, I'm sure. And you won't have to come very far. Just a mile or so from Scorpio House. And I've got a terrific beachfront. Russ can confirm that. Come on! It'll be great fun!"

Holly returned his smile. She had to confess this was exactly the sort of invitation she'd often dreamed of when she'd been trapped in Norris Falls. "I haven't been swimming since I was a teenager. In fact, I can't really swim at all. Just float. But if you're sure I won't be laughed out of town by local Olympic contenders—"

"Never happen. Promise! Great! If there's anything you want to know, what to wear, who'll be there, anything like that, here's my number." Kyle extracted a business card from his wallet and passed it to her. "Call me any time. My answering service will get it to me if I'm not available right then, and I'll get back to you. That's a promise, too. Guaranteed! Anytime, for a call from *you*."

Russ Graham toyed with a slice of pizza, listening intently to the exchange. Sensing that scrutiny, Kyle suddenly became ill at ease, as if he'd broken some rule of male protocol. Scooting back his chair, he said, "I won't wear out my welcome, or Russ will break my neck. And I wouldn't blame him! I'll keep in touch. Let you know all the details as I get them ironed out. Okay? Russ?"

His hand was out again. Apparently he needed a lot of reassurance that the feud was truly over. With a mild snort of disdain, Russ took his hand.

"Be seeing you both. But I know three's a crowd, and Russ cut me out tonight. But next time, Princess, next time . . ." and he hurried back to his mother's circle.

Holly felt a trifle as though she'd stumbled onto the set of a soap opera. Kyle acted and spoke as if he and Russ were rivals for her affection. She barely knew either of them! Only this morning she'd been homeless and rootless. Now this. And all of it happening in a borrowed dress!

"Would you like a drink?" Russ asked.

"What? Oh. Well, maybe a beer. That goes good with pizza."

"Right. If you don't mind, I'll have something a trifle stronger." He beckoned to a server, consulted Holly again, ordered a German import for her and then rye whiskey for himself. As the waiter left, Holly was startled to see that Russ was clenching and unclenching his fists. He was like a volcano trying to suppress an eruption. In a strained tone, he said, "Please understand. This isn't a sophomoric attempt to get you intoxicated so I can take advantage of you. Nor do I intend to get drunk and disgusting. I just need something to take the edge off."

"Of course," she said, sympathetic. This wasn't at all like her father's occasional binges, before sickness put alcohol forever off-limits to him. If ever a man was entitled to a stiff drink, it was Russ Graham, after that near-fatal incident on the Tollway and now this tense encounter with Kyle. When the drinks arrived, she expected the artist to bolt the contents of the glass. Instead, he sipped it slowly, spacing it out with bites of pizza.

Holly did the same with her beer.

After a while, the palpable tension surrounding Russ began to fade away. He made polite conversation. Did Holly like the pizza? Would she like another drink? Would she care to dance? She declined the offer with thanks, pointing out that the floor was so jammed it was impossible to really "dance" out there. Russ went on, shifting topics. Did she know that the Martins operated one of Chicago's top art galleries? They'd given him his first one-man show. He mentioned other people in Dark Lake, expanding her knowledge about Bianca's new friends considerably.

Relaxed, uncomplicated chit chat, seemingly designed to put Holly at ease. It was a side of this moody man that she hadn't expected. Or . . . was it a façade? Hard to say. She suspected she'd seen several, and by no means all, of the facets of Graham's personality. At times he showed a frank, flattering interest in her as a woman. At others, an undercurrent of deep sadness. At still others, a barely leashed rage. It certainly made "reading" him a challenge!

For some months past, Holly had had to be a nurse. It was a lousy job, but she'd proved more than capable at it. There was little she could do to stop physical and emotional disaster from dragging her father down. But she'd done her best to give him comfort during the terrible descent. Now, sensing Russ Graham's inner turmoil, she felt drawn to help him, if that was possible.

And yet . . . a nagging imp hovered at the back of her mind, whispering warnings, repeating gossip. *Alanna Preis—murdered. And he was her lover, wasn't he?*

She seemed to hear Maud saying, *"It looked so bad for Russ for a while—with Kyle gone and Russ finding her body like that."*

Like that. Bloodily dead from multiple stab wounds.

Little wonder it had taken the two men involved with Alanna a year to get to the stage of merely shaking hands. And little wonder Russ Graham now nursed a potent drink, trying to blot out terrible memories.

Holly was caught in her own tangle of emotions—intrigued by all the masculine attentions she'd enjoyed today, and badly rattled by the thread connecting the men, a thread leading straight back to murder.

She wasn't awake and she wasn't asleep. Holly drifted in a kind of limbo, not willing to rouse herself to full wakefulness.

Not willing . . . or not able?

Images blurred in her unconscious mind, flaring and fading.

It was delicious to lie abed and dream, wasn't it? No thoughts of duty or obligation. The sensation was a trifle sinful . . .

Darkness, and then, sudden light, as if a door had snapped open. And outlined in the doorway—a figure: large, featureless, menacing.

Who was it? A man, certainly. There was no mistaking the male physique—broad shoulders and narrow hips. But *who?*

And then another image, superimposed atop the first. An immense, sinuous, inhuman shape. A scorpion! No, a *symbol*: the astrological sign of Scorpio.

70

The male figure, shielded in blackness, moving forward, raising his arm. He was holding something long and pointed. As he lifted it above his head it reflected the light shining behind him. Such a gleam could only come from metal.

Sharp, pointed . . . a knife!

Over-limned by the scorpion, the figure advanced toward her, his hand descending in a deadly arc, stabbing . . .

Holly's hands flew to her mouth as a shriek tried to tear itself up out of her throat. She sat bolt upright, eyes wide with terror.

She was in bed. Alone. It was morning. There was no doorway, no darkened room, no silhouetted figure, and no knife.

But above her a narrow streak of sunlight lay across the ceiling of her room.

The window drapes didn't quite meet, and a sliver of daylight peeped through the small gap. That radiance flashed thinly onto the ceiling, creating an unnerving illusion of a blade.

There was a sharp knock at the door. Bianca called out, "Hey, Slugabed! Are you awake yet?"

Holly's first attempt to reply brought only a rasping croak. She swallowed and finally managed to say, "Yes. Come in."

Her sister sailed into the room bearing a breakfast tray, setting it on the bedside table. "Lazybones! Here it is almost noon and you're still dead to the world." Bianca tossed back the drapes. Full sunshine flooded the room. "Up and doing, now."

Sunshine. Bianca. Reality.

Holly shook her head to jar loose sleep cobwebs and memories of a horrid, vivid dream. "Have a heart, Sis. I'm entitled to sleep in after all the months when I had to get up at the

71

crack of dawn to fix Dad's medicine. And you *know* I'm not used to staying up till four in the morning." Bianca ignored her complaints and transferred the tray to the bed, fussing over its placement. Holly frowned and said, "What's this? Don't you have maids to do this sort of thing?"

Her sister made a deprecating noise. "Nothing's too good for my baby sister. Besides, I thought it would be nice—just the two of us."

Holly eyed the tray, hoping Bianca hadn't done the cooking—because unless Stephen Detloff could work absolute miracles, Bianca was a disaster in the kitchen.

The food looked more than presentable, though. And smelled delicious. "Mm! Sausage, hash browns, pineapple juice, Earl Grey . . . all my favorites. This is great."

A startling thought hit her: Stephen had chosen the room's décor, predicting its occupant's taste with uncanny accuracy. Had he . . . ? "Did . . . did Stephen pick this menu?"

"Don't be silly! Astrology can't tell him things like *that!*"

"Then how—"

"Oh, I remembered, from when we were kids. And during the preparations for the funeral, you said something that reminded me of the things you liked to eat." Bianca tried to sound offhanded, but it was plain that she was proud of her new-found concern for her sister's comfort. Holly forked up some hash browns, sighed in contentment, and dug in. Bianca perched on the edge of the bed and demanded, "Now tell me all about last night."

"What do you mean? We went to the same places."

"Oh, but I was with Stephen. Safe old married woman," Bianca said with a giggle. "You were being fought over by two of the most eligible bachelors in the Region. We all saw them shaking hands. Did they really kiss and make up. Tell all!"

Holly found she couldn't be annoyed. Bianca was like an

excited kitten. "The experience was certainly a world apart from all those months of reading war stories to Father, or watching idiot dramas on TV."

"Which do you like best? They're both so good looking!"

Holly stirred her tea and took a long, indulgent sip before replying. "Bianca, I just met them. I don't make snap judgments. Before I go any further, I need to know a *lot* more about those men."

"Like what?" Bianca was more than eager to please—and to be in on the ground floor of any gossip-generating developments.

"Well, their backgrounds, for starters. They seem to be very different in all sorts of ways. Makes me wonder how they ended up in Dark Lake living less than a mile from each other. That sort of thing." Holly washed down a bite of sausage with some Earl Grey and waited.

"Mm. Okay. Let's see. Kyle's family's lived in the Region forever, from what Stephen told me. Grandfather Preis owned a small newspaper syndicate and kept on expanding. But Kyle's father—Dan—got into serious financial difficulty several years ago. Bad investments, or trouble with one of his employees embezzling funds, or something like that. Anyway, Dan was working together with Stephen to solve the problems. That made good sense, of course; I mean, Stephen's been one of Preis Enterprises' top moneymakers, you know," Bianca said, beaming with pride. "But before they could get it all straightened out, Dan was killed in a terrible one-car accident." A look of uncertainty came over her lovely face. "Maud said there were suspicions."

Alarms jangled along Holly's nerve endings. "Suspicions?"

"That . . . well . . . that it might really have been suicide. Nothing was ever proved. I mean, the police and insurance

73

investigators didn't file any charges or anything like that. But there were plenty of people in the community who suspected Dan might have taken that way out. To spare his family. He could have been so despondent over the company's finances that he . . . well, his friends *did* have their doubts. At any rate, it solved the money problems. I guess the company's handling its debts okay, at least for now. And Sylvia's certainly been living it up on Dan's insurance ever since the accident," Bianca finished with disgust.

"I can't imagine how Kyle's father—or *any* man—ever wanted to marry that woman," Holly said, shaking her head. "Maybe she was a sweet-tempered doll in her salad days and only changed as she got older?"

Her sister shrugged. "Maybe. I do know that Stephen says she wasn't quite so hard to take when Kyle was a kid. But after Dan died, and after Kyle started declaring his independence . . ."

"That fits a pattern. Makes you feel sorry for him, doesn't it?" Holly took a sip of juice, thinking. "All right. I've got a better handle on Mr. Kyle Preis now. What about Mr. Russell Graham?"

Her sister leaned back and took a deep breath. "Whew! As you said, *very* different. Again, realize everything I'm telling you I picked up from Stephen, with some extras from Maud . . ."

"Dark Lake's mother hen and professional gossip. Yes, I know. Go on."

"Well, apparently Russ's family was dirt poor. Appalachia and all that. In fact, Maud says he's an orphan, grew up on handouts from his cousins in West Virginia, or somewhere like that. He joined the service when he was barely old enough to enlist—"

"Service?" Holly interrupted. Visions flashed through her

mind, a universe of images gleaned from listening to her father's cronies and to vets who'd matriculated at Holly's university. A lot of those stories had been heavily shadowed with the awful violence associated with active military service. Had Russ Graham been in active service? Bianca probably wouldn't know that sort of detail.

Confirming that guess, her sister went on, "Mm hm. I don't know which branch he joined or what kinds of assignments he was given. Maud thinks it was mainly a duty thing for him, not a career move. You know, doing his job for Uncle Sam. After he was discharged, he entered art school. Apparently Russ had been interested in art since he was a little kid. His military bonus allowed him to get the education he wanted."

Holly nodded. "That makes sense." Despite her comment, she couldn't shake off a vision of Russ Graham wearing covert operation gear, knives and firearms at the ready, setting forth on some deadly mission. Hoping for further elaboration, she raised an eyebrow, asking, "And?"

"Well, that's it. He graduated, worked a while for a Chicago graphics company, and did lots of freelancing. The Martins spotted his talent and tipped off Stephen, who gave him his first really big commercial break. And ever since, I guess Russ has been doing pretty well for himself. Enough background?"

"It'll do, thanks. But I'm still not going to make up my mind about either of them in any kind of hurry, so don't sit there panting with impatience. What was it Father used to say when we were kids? 'Slowly, slowly, catchee monkey'? " Her sister grimaced in annoyance. Chuckling, Holly went on, "But I *will* give you this little tidbit for your gossip fests: Kyle invited us to a swimming party on the fourth."

"Oh, yes. Stephen says that's an annual event with Kyle."

Then Bianca took in the full import of the news. "Us? You mean you and me and Stephen?"

"I assume you'll be included. But I meant Russ and me."

"He invited *Russ?* But that's just wonderful! Wait'll I tell Maud and Cynth. They'll be so delighted. It's been such nonsense, the two men not—"

"I know," Holly said. Her sister's eyes widened as she went on, "It wasn't a scandal I could avoid hearing. I *do* wish you'd tipped me off in advance, before I found out about the murder from others."

Bianca pouted prettily. "Oh, what does that matter? It's nothing that will ever affect us."

"No more than it affected Alanna Preis? Bianca, it affected those two men. And if I continue to see them, it'll affect me. No evading the situation. Maud told me about the Butcher Knife Murderer, how he's still on the loose and we have to be on guard—"

"How?" Bianca asked with callous practicality.

Holly had to admit that was a key point. How *did* one guard against a murderer even the police couldn't apprehend? And how could an unskilled, helpless woman do anything to defend herself against such a vicious menace? "All the same, I wish you'd told me . . ."

"Oh, let's not talk about it," Bianca said, sweeping the subject under the rug. "Stephen wants to see you. So finish your breakfast and get dressed, Pet."

Holly recalled her brother-in-law's urgent request last night—that she must talk to him privately. "What about?"

"I'm not sure, but he said you weren't the type to sit around and eat chocolates and watch television. Something about your Virgo Moon. He said he was going to find a challenge for you."

"He's right about my not wanting to waste my time. But

then, he usually is, isn't he?" Holly murmured, eyeing Bianca with a smile.

"Don't be snide!" her sister retorted with sudden heat, surprising Holly. Bianca went on the defensive. "Yes, he *is* usually right. He's a genius! If you don't appreciate that yet, you will. He's the most marvelous . . ." She paused, a little embarrassed by her ferocious defense of her husband. Gracefully, the former model rose and straightened her lustrous off-white tunic over her matching slacks. "Will it be okay if I make you an appointment with my hairdresser, say early next week? And we'll go shopping for some clothes, too. If . . . if that's all right with you?" Her manner turned coaxing, almost pleading.

Holly stared at her sibling, amazed by this new aspect of Bianca's personality.

Where were the usual steamroller tactics? All her life, Holly had coped with Bianca's habit of making plans without bothering to consult her or find out what Holly truly wanted.

Stephen Detloff must be teaching her to be gracious and patient. *Something* certainly had made radical changes to the sisters' relationship, and all for the better, from Holly's point of view.

"Sounds fine, and thanks for the offer. I know I've . . . well, let myself slide. I just didn't have the heart for it, or the money to spare, or the leisure to go shopping."

"Well, I'll help you make up for lost time, Pet. And you'll just adore Jerry's salon." Bianca bent forward and planted a noisy kiss on Holly's cheek. "Speaking of shopping, I have some to do. See you later," she said and dashed out of the bedroom.

Holly muttered, "At least, this time, she gave me warning before she dumped me in the nine-foot level. And I am in familiar surroundings . . . sort of." She peered around the room, once more relishing the color scheme and luxurious appointments. Cinderella of Norris Falls, now Princess of Dark Lake. A woman could get used to such pampering, and quickly, too. All this, and breakfast in bed! Holly dug in, savoring every morsel.

An hour later, though, wandering through the hallways and rooms of Scorpio House, she wondered if she'd ever get used to her new environment. Stephen's castle-that-astrology-built was huge and disturbingly empty. She neither saw nor heard servants and might have been alone in a magician's fortress.

Holly made her way down to the living room. The black velvet drapes had been drawn back to admit sunlight through floor-to-ceiling window walls. She speculated there must have been servants around to perform that task, at least. Her shoes sank into the carpeting as she crossed the area. The piano in the corner drew her like a magnet.

Holly touched the keys, running an arpeggio remembered from childhood lessons.

Wistful, she hoped Stephen wouldn't mind if she played now and then.

Stephen. Where *was* Stephen Detloff? Where was everybody, for that matter?

Searching, Holly went through a door leading off the far end of the living room and walked down a corridor. Dark wood, dark paneling—like a tunnel. In the distance, she heard voices. Ah! Life signs at last!

At the end of the corridor she found an office, or perhaps a receptionist's cubby, except that no one was on duty. There were filing cabinets and a desk—clean of clutter but adorned by a small pot of ivy. A few comfortable chairs sat at strategic points around the little room. Astrological paintings—more of Russ Graham's work?—hung on the walls. A gigantic horoscopic chart covered the space behind the desk.

Holly assumed this was the gateway to Stephen's main work area, the place where he dispensed advice to his clients. But where was *he?*

Then she heard his voice, that unmistakable sorcerer's intonation. The words came through a slightly ajar door to her right. "Under present aspects, I see very little that is encouraging, I'm afraid. After mid-August, matters are likely to change for the better. And always remember: These are only indications, a map to point out possible pitfalls. You can rise above malign influences if you marshal the spiritual strength from within. And you will need that strength, dear friend. Your Pluto continues to plague your chart, promising violent upheaval and unexpected setbacks, perhaps even personal danger. Mars warns of an enemy, someone you least expect. And with Uranus at your Midheaven, we may anticipate a crisis of lifestyle which may alter your entire future irrevocably. The next few weeks will be absolutely critical . . ."

His voice was mesmerizing, turning each phrase into the pronouncements of an infallible oracle. Holly felt hair rising on the back of her neck.

"With Saturn in your third house, my dear, we must be prepared for feelings of guilt and depression. And since it is on the cusp, this will probably be associated in some way with your parents or your home. You must fight the temptation to give into sorrow and moodiness. Become involved with others. And above all, protect yourself. I don't want to alarm you, but there is danger in your prospects. Possible injury, even death, and these are in some way connected with affairs of the heart. I wish I could be more specific, but I cannot. Beware the cloak of friendship and love, my dear. Beware!"

Holly was rooted where she stood. Astrology was a pseudoscience, wasn't it?

But Stephen's words had a frightening ring of truth. He'd been right so often.

Who was the subject of that grim forecast? Who was in dire danger? Had she overheard someone else's terrible horoscope . . . or her own?

Chapter 5

As wild speculations rattled in her mind, Holly noticed a movement at the door. She edged forward slowly and peered into the room beyond. Kyle Preis, his back to her, stood a few yards away. He was asking someone, "You sure that's the right address?"

Toby Carmichael scooted into view, skillfully maneuvering his desk chair between towering units of electronic equipment. "I'm sure. What's the matter? Don't you think I know my job?"

"Aww, don't take it so personally. I just needed to double-check before I made any calls . . ."

Holly realized she was still hearing Stephen Detloff's voice, although his words were now overridden by those of Kyle and Toby. Comprehension burst upon her. A wall full of miniature TV screens and speakers were running—flickering lights, fluctuating gauges, needles and meters jumping with each syllable Stephen spoke.

Recordings! Some of the astrologer's popular, ubiquitous programs. Toby must be making copies of his interviews. She'd heard one from the other room, and misinterpreted. That *wasn't* the voice of doom pronouncing her own fate!

She could kick herself for being so stupid and gullible. Had she dared call herself a skeptic about astrology and the occult? Here she was leaping to melodramatic conclusions and scaring herself silly over nothing!

Kyle scribbled an address on a Palm Pilot and turned to

leave. Delight bloomed on his handsome face when he saw Holly. "Well, hello!" He was dressed for a business meeting—dark suit, silk tie, the works. "Damn! I wish I weren't heading back to Chicago so soon. I'd love to take you for a drive around the lake today and give you a guided tour of my place. Rain check?"

"Certainly. Actually, I wouldn't even be here in the offices, except Bianca said Stephen wants to talk to me."

"Sooner or later we all end up talking to Stephen, don't we? In case you hadn't already guessed, our Lord Scorpio is actually a sun. He's the central body in our entire Dark Lake social circle. We all revolve around him. Or should that be 'rotate'?" Kyle said with a lopsided grin.

"Orbit," Toby corrected him, not looking up. He was searching through a messy pile of papers, his expression bitter.

"Whatever," the publisher muttered, ignoring the interruption. He took Holly's hand and rubbed his thumb caressingly across her fingers. Something in his manner made her doubt that he was even aware of what he was doing. He might have been daydreaming, his mind a million miles away. His touch was simultaneously soothing and stimulating. Had he used the same caress to charm Alanna? Holly hastily shut down that line of thought.

Waking from mental wandering, Kyle said, "You haven't forgotten about the fourth, have you?" He sounded hopeful, little-boy eager.

"No, I haven't forgotten. I'm looking forward to it. Bianca and I are going shopping tomorrow. I'll be sure to buy a swimsuit." He brightened still further, beaming down at her. She realized from his reaction that she must have adopted, quite unconsciously, what Bianca called her "all-knowing, Mona Lisa look." Apparently it really *was* an effective flirting technique.

"You aren't looking forward to the party half as much as I am," Kyle promised, his thumb still busy on her fingers. An odd look crossed his features—that of a youngster caught with his hand in the cookie jar and fearing Mama would spank him. Then he sighed and said, "Oh, hell! If I don't get moving, I'll never get to my appointment on time. Remember now, Princess—the fourth. With bells on!"

He bent and kissed her cheek, then dashed out. Absently, Holly touched the spot his lips had brushed. Was this part of the "beautiful people" routine? Probably in Kyle's world a peck like that meant no more than a handshake. Just the same . . .

"Watch your step, Miss Frey. He's an expert heart-breaker," Toby warned, employing almost the same phrase Maud had. Stephen's man-of-all-work continued pawing through the stack of papers, increasingly annoyed that he couldn't find what he sought.

"He seems . . . very nice," Holly said carefully. A safe statement, surely. Completely non-committal. She turned her attention to Toby's machines, awed by the array. It looked like something that ought to be in CIA HQ or NORAD. Holly had never seen so many computers and recording devices crammed together in one space.

Now that she knew what this was all about, she began to pick out other ongoing interviews and conversations. Muted voices purred from the speakers. One reproduced a TV chat with a world-famous actress noted for her unique and affected performances. Another was distinctive for his strong Middle European accent, one that Holly recalled from newscasts; the man was a powerful politician in his own country.

Now and then Toby reached out and touched a switch or cued a key, never raising his eyes from his search pattern over the papers. In his own way, he was as much of a wizard as Stephen Detloff.

Holly cocked her head, zeroing in on one particular interview. She heard a woman's anxious voice asking questions and Stephen's mesmerizing answering analysis. Through the magic of electronics, Toby was preserving a past conversation between his boss and a troubled client. Holly hoped that client was less disturbed by Stephen's words than *she* had been minutes ago!

Gasping in irritation, Toby shoved aside the stack of papers. It toppled to one side, worsening the mess. He leaned back in his chair and said, "Welcome to Scorpio's inner sanctum—recordings and preservations department."

"You do all of this alone?" she said, shaking her head in wonderment.

"At the moment, yes. Plus handling the receptionist's desk, in there." He nodded, rather than pointed, at yet another connecting door to an adjacent office. "Or at least I try," Toby went on. "It's really not my bag. Normally, his secretary takes care of that end, and all the paper filing," he added, glowering at the sprawl across his work space. "But she got married and moved to California. So I'm helping out. Or attempting to." He paused and frowned. "You're here to see Stephen, right? He's on the phone with a VIP right now. As soon as he's free, I'll let him know you're here." He leaned forward and tapped a particular red light on one machine. Holly assumed that was Stephen's BUSY signal.

"Aren't all of them VIPs?" Holly asked, gesturing to the banks of electronic equipment.

"No, not all of them. He does a lot of . . . I guess you could sort of call it an astrologer's version of *pro bono*. Cut-rate for clients who don't have big bucks. Gives them good service, though," Toby said proudly. "Nobody gets shoddy predictions from him, I guarantee."

"At first, I thought he was in here." Holly glanced toward the screen where the ominous interview was replaying. Stephen's deep voice issued more loudly from that speaker than any other.

Toby grinned. "When I get through, you'll think that one's broadcasting live. Stephen can show up dozens of places at once, thanks to these babies," and he patted the side of a unit. "Plus he's done a bunch of standard, pre-recorded 'instant horoscopes' for the easily satisfied customer. That's about eighty percent of 'em, truth to tell. It frees him up for consultations with the heavy hitters, the ones who pay mucho bucks for a few words from The Master."

Holly whistled. "And you do everything!"

"Yep. And if I do say so, I'm pretty good at it. I can set up systems for anybody. I did one for Preis Publishing, for example . . ."

"Maud said he—Kyle—played around with recordings. Compiling . . . well . . . I guess you'd call them embarrassing playbacks."

Toby winced. "Yeah. I heard about that. Sometimes I'm damned sorry I taught him so many tricks of the trade. If he wanted to buckle down and work at it, he'd be almost as good as I am. It's been quite a while since I installed that setup at his office and Mama Sylvia's. I wonder if he's changed any of it—"

A soft beep issued from the unit with the red light. Toby pressed a switch and said, "Yes, sir?"

"Please be sure to mark Kyle's Fourth of July party on my calendar, won't you? Mrs. Detloff is counting on it so." This time, Holly knew it was the *real* Stephen talking.

"I'll attend to it right away," the tech expert promised, scribbling on a clipboard.

Stephen's voice stopped, but the red light stayed on. Holly guessed that meant the astrologer was still busy. As Toby finished his note, she said, "Are you going to the party, too?" Pain tightened his elfin face and she quickly added, "I'm sorry. I didn't mean to hit a nerve."

"Very perceptive of you—to notice that *did* hit. Shall we just say it's an old wound that doesn't bear talking about and leave it at that? I'll probably receive an invitation, but I won't be going."

Holly nodded, took a breath, hoping she wouldn't step on his toes again, and said, "Russ Graham asked me to give you a message. He said he had a visitor he wanted you to meet."

"Oh?" Toby's expression lightened. He seemed intrigued.

At that moment the red light went off. Toby again touched a key switch and informed his boss that Holly was waiting. Then he jumped to his feet and hurried to open the door of still another adjoining room. Apparently this led to a shortcut, avoiding the reception area. The private entrée implied Holly ranked highly on Stephen's schedule.

Stephen's office was huge. The astrologer sat behind an ebony desk, teetering back and forth in an executive chair. As Holly came in, he got up and in an elaborate, courtly fashion, saw her seated comfortably. "Forgive the delay, my dear. I had to make some money," and he chuckled deprecatingly. "I must keep my beautiful Bianca in the style to which she should be accustomed. And I have to keep all of this functioning," he said, sweeping an arm around to indicate the complex of offices. "Did Bianca tell you why I wanted to see you?"

"Not exactly. Something about knowing I wouldn't want to be idle."

Her brother-in-law tapped a long finger against his lips, studying her with a calculating stare, a sculptor looking over a lump of clay. "I have a proposition, quite an honest one, I promise. As soon as I saw the Neptune in your chart, I immediately decided on this plan of action."

"Beg pardon?" Holly blurted. Then she understood. Astrology. Again.

"Ah! Your skeptical Taurean elements are in play once more, I see. And yet, we can help each other, Holly. You, a non-believer in the occult, and I, the occultist in desperate need of help." He spoke with the fervor of an evangelist.

She smiled and said carefully, "I'm listening."

"It occurred to me that you'd feel somewhat restless if you didn't have work to occupy your time. You are most definitely service-oriented. I'd have known that without consulting a chart, simply by what my dear Bianca has told me. Your devotion to your father, putting aside your own employment at the university branch office, selflessly—"

"I'm not a saint," Holly protested, the heat of a blush warming her face. "He . . . he needed me. And . . . well, I suppose I've always felt a child owed something to the parent who put up with so much when that child was young. Father . . . became a child, in a way, and I wanted to be there for him."

"Even though your task was bitter and little appreciated by its beneficiary."

"I didn't say that."

Stephen shook his head solemnly. "No, you didn't. But it's true, nonetheless. You are definitely a service-oriented person, my dear. Don't deny it. Would that there were many, many more of your sort in the world. For what you've endured . . . let me see. How did Bianca put it? That you have a perfect right to be repaid for your sacrifices."

Holly bit her tongue before she could spit out an angry comment.

Stephen read her reaction like a book, his manner very gentle. "Please be patient with her, my Aquarian friend. It's true she often has allowed herself to be limited by juvenile elements of her personality. But I assure you, her potential is truly magnificent. Trust me! With the proper nurturing guidance, she will undergo changes that will truly astound you. This I guarantee. She has a fine Cancerian soul, one ready to evolve to a much higher level. And you and I shall help that to happen. Love her, if you can find it in your heart. I beg you."

Holly was tempted to say that Stephen was far too good for her sister, and that she couldn't imagine what such a sophisticated man saw in a flighty fashion plate. But something in his tone made her swallow those words. Was this "evolution" he spoke of possible? She had to admit she'd already noticed alterations in Bianca's behavior. If these were Stephen's doing . . .

"Of course I'll love her. I always have. It's just that a great deal of the time I find it extremely difficult to *like* her."

"That will change, that will change." Stephen sat up straight and looked at his guest intently. "Now, to business. Would you consider entering my employ, Holly?"

She hastily rearranged her train of thought. If this offer had come from Bianca, she would have suspected a throwing-crumbs-to-the-hopeless gesture. But it had come from Stephen . . .

"What . . . what did you have in mind?"

"Executive secretarial work, of a sort."

"Oh. Toby said your secretary got married and moved away."

"My secretary and Toby's as well. This has put an impossible burden on him. He needs to be free to take care of my computer correspondence and the electronic end of the business. That's a massive task. He shouldn't have to struggle with filing papers and keeping appointments straight," Stephen said, his expression fond.

"He seems very devoted to you."

"As I to him. Toby has been with me for years. He's stored up a heavy burden of unearned karmic debt in his short life, I fear. The least I can give him is the constancy of my friendship. Your job would be to take all those extra chores off his back. And mine! I confess I loathe filing and calendar keeping and such nonsense. But I suspect you enjoy it. Am I correct?"

"I do. Because it's in my chart?" Holly asked wryly. She felt odd. Stephen had hit the mark dead on. She did indeed like to organize things, even if only recipe files.

The astrologer's deep-set dark eyes twinkled. "It *is* in your chart. And if I'm reading you right, at the moment you're rather at loose ends. For months, you've been a loyal, hard working slave to duty, obedient to your filial obligation to a dying parent. You deserve a rest. But I suspect after the briefest of vacations, you'll start squirming and getting the fidgets if you don't have regular, useful work to put your hands to."

She gaped at him. This was uncanny. How could he dive so deeply into her psyche on such short acquaintance?

Stephen reached into a drawer and extracted a folder. He removed its contents and handed them to her. It was a horoscope—a twelve-partite wheel and several pages of analysis. At the top of the first page, in bold but neat printing, she read the words, "Holly Frey," her birth date, time, and the latitude and longitude of the hospital where she had first seen the world.

"I made that out when Bianca and I first met," he explained. "I asked her about her family, and I thought you might like a copy." His thin lips parted in a wide grin, re-vealing large white teeth. "Read it at your leisure, my dear."

"Th . . . thank you." Holly skimmed the pages, repressing a shiver. She folded the pages and slipped them in a pocket of her jeans. "I will. And I'll think over your offer of a job."

"Take your time. I can wait as long as I must," he said, nodding. "I confess that when I saw your chart my mouth fairly watered in anticipation. You're exactly what this office has needed. Your chart correlates perfectly with Toby's and mine. We'd make a superlative team."

"Would we?" she asked, forcing a shaky little smile.

"There is one thing," he cautioned. "You have Uranus over your Midheaven at present." Holly started, remem-bering that was what he'd noted in the woman celebrity's horoscope. Stephen went on, "This is a critical influence. It foretells great change in your life. Obviously, your father's death was part of that. And with aspects in the eighth and fourth houses . . ."

"Does my chart have anything to do with the sign of Scorpio?" Holly demanded suddenly.

"Why do you ask?" Stephen was very intent, leaning for-ward.

"Oh, nothing." She found she couldn't bring herself to talk about her dream.

"Mm. There are numerous signs in your chart that hint at a high degree of unconscious clairvoyance. I have that in my chart as well."

Was her dream a glimpse of her future? The symbol of Scorpio and the figure with the knife . . .

Stephen hurried around the desk and knelt before her, gripping her hands firmly. Holly felt lightheaded. Apparently she'd turned pale with fright, pale enough to alarm the astrologer. "Forgive me for saying such things!" he exclaimed. "I'm a stupid fool! I should have realized that someone with your progressed Saturn—"

"Please! No more horoscopes and charts and predications! Not for a while, at least."

"I apologize. Truly. But . . . I wanted you to be forewarned. I have a horror of innocents suffering through lack of knowledge, and if I can inform, if I can reach the subject in time to—" he broke off, closing his eyes in obvious emotional pain.

Was he thinking of Alanna Preis? Had Stephen's calculations shown that she was in danger? And did he blame himself for not warning *her* in time?

Her legs a bit rubbery, Holly got to her feet, grateful for Stephen's supporting arm. "I didn't mean to be such a baby. Normally, I'd take something like this in stride."

"I'm quite aware of that fact. This is all my fault."

"No, it's not." Holly's chin went up, her stubbornness gene kicking in. "But, just the same, I think I'd better go. I'm sure you have tons of work to catch up on, and I'm keeping you from it."

Her brother-in-law understood her desire for escape and courteously greased her exit route. He saw her to the door, his hand resting lightly on her elbow. "Please relax and make yourself completely at home here at Scorpio House, my dear. If you'd like to go shopping, ask Toby for a car. He'll supply you with keys. We have a variety of vehicles available for your use."

Holly thanked him and slipped outside. For a moment, she leaned against the closed door to his office, pulling herself together more thoroughly and taking deep breaths.

Back near the reception area, Toby Carmichael was busy on the phone and engrossed in writing down a message. Holly was grateful that he hadn't seen her when she first emerged from Stephen's inner sanctum. If he had, the computer expert would probably have guessed how upset she was, to her further chagrin. As he finished his call and swiveled his chair, she put on a calm face.

"Did everything go okay, Miss Frey?"

"Why, yes." To throw him off any scent of her fear, she chided, "If I can call you Toby, won't you call me Holly?"

With a shy smile he said, "Sure, if that's what you'd prefer. I didn't want to push informality too soon. It's . . . well . . . because I'm in kind of an ambiguous position—more than a hired hand, less than a member of the family."

"Stephen says you're his friend." Toby looked touched as she went on, "Do you live here at Scorpio House?"

"Yeah. Think that qualifies me as sort of family?"

"That, and a great deal more, from the way Stephen spoke of you," Holly assured him.

It was plain that her words pleased him enormously. His tentative smile had widened into a cheerful grin. Then he snapped his fingers and nodded to the notepad beside the phone. "Say, that was Russ who just called. You didn't mention that he'd asked you to drop in, too, when I walked over for a visit. Want to come along with me? I'm knocking off for a while. We could get some fresh air together."

Holly hesitated before asking, "Are you sure I'll be welcome? Last night I got the impression that Mr. Graham is rather . . . touchy."

"Hah! You hit that nail on the head. Stephen explained it to me once—said it had something to do with Russ's Scorpio Moon."

Holly suddenly felt cold. With anger, she shook off the reaction. She had to stop believing in all this astrological nonsense! This latest revelation about Russ had nothing to do with reality. Nor did ominous predictions, a terrifying dream, or her so-called unconscious clairvoyance!

"He's temperamental, yeah," Toby went on, seemingly unaware of her response to his earlier comment. "Artistic temperament, I guess. But when you get to know him, you'll learn to ignore him when he sulks. Trust me; you'll be welcome. He made a special point of repeating the invitation to you—and he doesn't do that very often, I guarantee," he finished, a teasing note in his voice.

"Well . . ." Holly glanced down at her jeans and t-shirt. "Should I change?"

"Nah, you're fine. Genuine Dark Lake casual, I'd call it. Let's go!"

She followed him along a corridor to a solarium. An exterior door there led out onto a flagstone terrace. Stepping into the sunlight, Holly blinked like a mole coming out of its nest. She cupped her hands above her brow until her eyes adjusted to the sudden change. The sky was a brilliant blue and sprinkled with low, wind-fluffed clouds. The air was heavy with the pleasant scent of green, growing things. It was as though they had entered a different world, leaving Stephen's dire predictions far behind.

"Good to be alive, isn't it?" Toby said with a chuckle. He led the way to a gate and the path beyond. The trail descended a gentle slope through the small woodland girdling Scorpio House. Spruce, oak, and juniper surrounded the walkers and towered over a carpet of wildflowers. Somewhere in a thicket a jay screamed, "Thief! Thief!"

"This is like a park," Holly exclaimed. "So cool and refreshing after all that heat and humidity yesterday. Nature's air conditioner—trees!" Toby chuckled and nodded.

She reveled in the scenery. It was a balm for troubled spirits. But she wished she'd worn sandals instead of tennies. The path was a mixture of packed soil and sand, and inevitably some of the grit got inside her shoes. Several times she had to ask Toby to stop while she removed a sneaker and shook out the accumulation.

"How far is it to Russ's?"

"Oh, about half a mile. You can see his place from the upper floors of Scorpio House, but the woods block your view from the street level."

Of course. Holly remembered now, Graham telling her how close he lived to Stephen, and how the information had disturbed her at the time. Here, amid this sylvan beauty, such fears seemed silly.

The two passed a birch grove and started down a crude stairway formed of split logs. Toby cautioned her to use the rope handrail. When they reached the bottom Holly said, "This is fun. Thank you for insisting that I come."

"You're welcome. Sometime you might want to try walking clear around the lake. It's only about three miles. Or you could use a bike; I think there's a couple in the garage. Lots of the locals bicycle. They claim it's good for the ecology, but I think they're just getting in cheap exercise and saving on gym fees."

There was a certain quality about Toby that intrigued Holly, something she couldn't quite put her finger on. She was sure she'd figure it out, though, in time. Her instincts on such matters had rarely betrayed her.

They finally emerged from the woods at the foot of a long slope. Before them lay Dark Lake's major road, a two-lane blacktop. Toby glanced both ways and was about to step out onto the pavement when he stopped abruptly. A mammoth car rounded the curve to his right, cruising toward the pair. It slowed to a halt and the driver's side window rolled down. Maud Rutherford leaned out and cried, "Oh, ho ho! Caught you, kiddies! What are you up to?"

Holly stared. She'd never seen such an enormous car.

She whispered to Toby, "I thought you said the locals used bicycles."

"I heard that! Can you see me on a bike, honey?" Maud laughed. She slapped a plump hand against the car's door. "I'll stick to my big old classic here. She's a genuine Checker." Returning to her first topic, she said, "Okay, 'fess up: Where you headed?"

"Just going over to Russ's, Miss Rutherford," Toby said.

"Hah!" Maud mugged outrageously and winked at Holly. "You sure don't waste time. I saw you in action last night, sweetie. Had both those guys wrapped around your little finger. And here you are, off at the crack of dawn to beard the artistic lion in his den!"

"Hardly the crack of dawn," Holly protested. Trying to shunt the exchange away from herself, she asked, "Are you out for an afternoon drive or an errand?"

"Oh, I'm always out and about somewhere. I'm a total perambulating type. Gotta keep tabs on everybody, you know. Well, Toby, you take real good care of this little girl, you hear? With all the wolves around, we have to keep a sharp eye on every new prospect who rolls into town. Ta ta, kids!" With that, she beeped the horn and moved off down the road at a leisurely pace.

"Does she do that often?" Holly said, staring after the enormous vehicle.

"Constantly. Finger in every pie, she calls it. Maud's a rule unto herself. No one knows where she might pop up next."

They crossed the now-empty road and picked up the trail again on the far side, meandering through a clover field. Dark Lake was visible ahead, though occasionally a dip in the path cut off their view of it. Beyond the field lay another small set of log steps, this one built into a sandy slope tamped with earth. Holly clutched the wooden banister, for the stairs were quite steep.

"Is this a blowout?" she wondered, gazing around. They were descending into an immense cup of sand. A few rotting stumps jutted above a barren landscape. Scattered, straggly patches of grass clung desperately to widely separated low dunes.

"You've seen a blowout before?" Toby asked with surprise.

"No, but I read about the area when Bianca married Stephen and moved here. The wind creates this sort of formation, doesn't it?"

"Blasts it out, you might say, given half a chance, even this far south of Lake Michigan, though we're not all that far away, come to that." Toby went on to explain, "This is the stable end of the blow. The other end is gradually eating its way toward Dark Lake. One of these years Russ is going to have a lakefront studio, whether he wants it or not."

She found the scene hauntingly beautiful. There was a feeling of eternity to the glacially spawned, wind-birthed blowout. It struck her as an inexorable reminder of Nature's permanence, that mankind was only a recent intruder across Earth's face.

The path was now paved with plankwood, which made walking a trifle easier. Even so, the constant wind displayed its power, trying to drift sand across the narrow walkway. In a few places, the wood was completely covered.

"What's that?" Holly said, pointing at a tall bench to one side of the path.

"Russ's target range." Toby indicated the sheer face of a sandy wall some yards beyond. Tattered paper targets hung from nails pounded into a wooden backstop built against the wall's face.

"Maud said he was a gun nut."

"Gun 'crank' is the correct term, or so I've been told. And there's his lair."

They had just passed a bushy clump of evergreens when Holly saw what Toby was talking about. A gravel driveway crossed the path and came to a dead end at an A-frame built against the blowout's rim. Russ Graham's Cherokee was parked beside the simple, utilitarian structure. A chattering, tapping noise issued from within the house. It took Holly a moment to identify the sound. A computer printer. That seemed odd, in this rather primitive setting.

Toby knocked at a door on the home's south side. He called loudly, "Anybody home?" A moment later Russ Graham appeared, unhooked the screen, and invited them in.

Holly examined the place with interest. Utilitarian indeed! It was as much a studio as a dwelling, with remarkably few concessions to creature comfort. There were a kitchenette, half bath, and storeroom built beneath a bedroom loft area to the right of the door. A small sofa, coffee table, and a few cabinets were arranged along the walls. But the center of the main floor was dominated by an easel and attendant tables cluttered with brushes, crumpled tubes of paint, sketchpads, palettes, and sheets of Masonite. A large northern window lighted the entire interior.

Russ Graham went to the storeroom adjoining the kitchenette and addressed someone within. "Knock it off for a while, huh? I'd like you to meet someone."

"Just a sec . . ." The printer stopped chattering and Holly heard a chair scraping the uncarpeted floor. Then a stocky young black man emerged from the nook. The stranger studied the visitors speculatively as Graham introduced them. "Holly is Stephen's sister-in-law, and Toby takes care of all his computer stuff. Toby, Holly, this is Ivor Wilcox, an old college buddy of mine. We bumped into each other at last month's book fair in Old Town. I think you and Ivor have a mutual acquaintance, Toby." The computer tech raised a questioning eyebrow. Russ grinned and went on, "Jesse Carpenter?"

He fell silent, watching the two men, Negro and blond, shaking hands and sizing one another up. The artist's expression was roguish and anticipatory.

The handshake went on and on. A slow smile bloomed on Ivor Wilcox's round face. Toby straightened, his elfin features alight.

Holly had heard of instant rapport but had never witnessed it until now. These two had taken to each other instantly. In fact, they seemed totally absorbed, unaware of her and Russ. Like the embrace between Stephen and Bianca, this encounter left Holly feeling vaguely embarrassed at being a witness.

"Jesse?" Toby said at last. "You know Jesse? Is he still with Ferris?"

"Oh, man, is he with Ferris! Lockstep. You'd think they were married!" Wilcox rubbed his free hand over his short-cut hair.

Suddenly, everything fell into place for Holly. Of course! If there *was* a gay community in Norris Falls, it had remained subterranean. But there were numerous homosexuals among Holly's classmates when she'd attended college. She mentally kicked herself for being so obtuse. Clairvoyant? Hah! Her "intuition" should have picked up on this much sooner, surely!

The men definitely had "clicked" and were chatting eagerly, exchanging names, dates, events, locations. Their enthusiasm grew by the second as they discovered how similar their tastes were and how many friends they had in common.

After long moments of noisy conversation, Wilcox suddenly said, "Hey, all this can't interest Russ and the lady. What say we cut out? I need to get cigs, anyway. How about you show me around Dark Lake? I'm gonna be working here for the next few months, so I need to know the layout, right? Russ, borrow your keys?" Apparently the artist expected the request. He had his key ring ready, tossing it to Wilcox. Ivor and Toby made hasty farewells and banged out the door. A moment later Russ's Cherokee tore past the window in a spray of sand, heading up the drive toward the blacktop road.

"That worked out well," Graham said with a satisfied chuckle. He began wiping paintbrushes on a rag. Holly decided her clothes weren't too sloppy, after all; the artist wore a paint-smeared, torn, and sleeveless sweatshirt and badly stained and faded jeans.

"They certainly hit it off," she agreed. "I gather you're playing matchmaker?"

His intense gaze darted her way. "In a way, I suppose I am. Toby's been on the loose—and on a downer—for some time. And Ivor went through a bad bust-up last year. A *real* bad one. He's just started to come out of it, so I thought I'd do the Samaritan bit." He paused and eyed her thoughtfully. "I must say you're taking this well. A lot more casually than I expected. I thought you were a small town girl—"

"That means quaint old-fashioned costumes and attitudes to match, right?" Holly said with heavy sarcasm. "Sorry to disappoint you. Did you really believe I'd turn Toby and your friend over to some Bible Belt vigilante lynching society?"

"No, I was pretty sure you wouldn't do that." The smug certainty in his statement irritated her further.

"Then why . . . ?"

"Forget it." Then, in a complete shift of topic, he said, "I've got to use up these acrylics before they get too dry. I won't be long. Help yourself to some iced tea or beer or what-ever. Make yourself at home."

With barely managed courtesy, Holly said, "Thank you." To his back. He was ignoring her, already at his easel, painting rapidly, as if trying to meet a deadline.

She shook her head tiredly, took him at his word, and went into the kitchenette. Further conversation wasn't a good idea, anyway, until she cooled off a trifle. Besides, it might disturb the artist's concentration.

Sipping an icy drink, Holly took the opportunity to look around. The house certainly reflected Graham's personality. Furnishings were sturdy and plain. A dozen firearms hung from racks lining the paneled walls. Such décor didn't bother her; she had been around her father and his vet cronies often enough while they talked about firearms. Like several of them, Russ Graham was apparently a so-called gun crank, a collector, and, judging by the target range outside, a shooter. It was a manly hobby. Plus, someone with Graham's temper probably needed a physical and noisy activity like that to blow off steam after an intense day of artistic endeavors.

Continuing her survey of the premises, Holly went into the storeroom, edging past boxes filled with paintings. Cans of thinner, canvas stretchers, and other artistic impedimenta filled shelving lining the walls. At the moment, the small area was also serving as guest quarters; a bedroll on a cot sat be-side a card table holding a laptop and a printer. Wilcox's pos-sessions, she assumed.

Curious, remembering the *Aquarius* painting in her bed-room, Holly began flipping idly through the pictures in the storage crates. Still somewhat irked by Graham's comments, she was prepared to be harshly critical about his work. How *dare* he believe she'd be shocked by Toby's sexual orientation!

But the paintings quickly wiped away her annoyance. This

man was truly talented. And versatile. It appeared that he sold in a wide variety of markets, using many different techniques and media. Pictures of sleek, futuristic autos stood beside Peter Max–style toys. A knight confronted a dragon. A hard-boiled detective and a gangster's moll confronted each other; that one, surely, was a cover for a mystery novel. There were also a lot of astrological themes designed to decorate Stephen Detloff's publications.

Everything she saw was thoroughly professional, and very solid. Yet Russ had been at pains to stress that he was a *commercial* artist. Holly recalled the gratitude in his voice when he said the Martins had staged his first one-man show. Did he yearn to be known as more than a "mere" commercial artist? Perhaps he longed to be a Rembrandt, as clowns supposedly itched to play Hamlet. Well, he deserved such appreciation. The man was *good*.

Holly bent to examine one particular painting more closely. She lifted it out of the crate and admired it. It was a portrait of a young woman, luminously real, appealing, and with an exquisitely lovely face and winsome smile. A cascade of black hair spilled across her shoulders and curled about her white throat. Her pale green gown matched the color of her eyes. This was what art was all about—capturing the soul of a living being. The subject of this picture was the essence of desirable womanhood, and, thanks to Russ Graham's genius, she was now immortal and eternal.

"Put that down!"

Holly jumped, shocked by that thunderous growl erupting right behind her. She was so startled she almost dropped the picture.

Russ Graham's fingers bit into the flesh of her upper arm. He jerked her around to face him. A palette knife, curiously held, like a dagger, was clutched in his free hand.

And his expression! Had she thought his pale blue eyes were fiery? Now they were lumps of radioactive material, lasing at her with fury.

Chapter 6

Holly struggled, trying to wrest her arm out of his grasp. "Let me go!" she cried, and got ready to kick his shins. She wasn't sure if that would be enough to make him release her, but she had to do something!

He blinked and glanced down, seeming to realize for the first time that he was holding her. As if stung, he let go so abruptly that Holly staggered a moment before she regained her balance.

Graham took the painting from her now-limp fingers. The fire in his eyes was dying to a smolder. "Sorry," he muttered. He didn't *sound* sorry, in Holly's opinion, but the man *was* visibly shifting to a lower emotional gear. "I didn't mean to . . . sorry."

He held the picture carefully, his expression tortured, as if the very sight of the painting hurt. Then, with a shudder, Graham slammed the portrait face down on a shelf.

"I . . . I didn't mean it," he repeated. "I didn't mean to hurt you. I honestly didn't."

His words sounded totally sincere. Then, without warning, he spun away from Holly and hurled the palette knife with all his strength. It skittered across the floor, bouncing and slamming to a stop at the base of the refrigerator. Graham pressed a fist to his mouth and sank his teeth into the knuckles.

Shaken, awash in his anguish, Holly blurted, "Whatever I did to cause this . . . *I'm* sorry. Truly. Please, let me help. Could I get you some water?"

Graham shook his head violently, rejecting the offer, struggling for self-control.

He moved out into the main room, a bit unsteady on his feet, acting like a drunken man. Groaning, he sat heavily on the sofa, his burning stare locked on nothing.

Taking the initiative, Holly went to the fridge and scanned its contents. As she expected, there were several cans of beer. She popped one and brought it to him, insisting he drink it. Graham didn't seem aware of her nagging for a while, then, listlessly, he accepted the can and began sipping.

Awed by the tempest she had inadvertently triggered, Holly sat in the chair beside him. After a long moment, she said, "Would . . . would you like to talk about it?"

Finally, he turned to look at her, his gaze clear at last. His pale eyes were soft, the fire gone out of them. "I hope your father appreciated you," he said, "if you were like this with him. You said he was demented, violent. Like me?"

"No. Yes," Holly replied, shaken by bad memories. "He suffered from fantasies, part of the time. Mostly paranoia. Such as believing his illness was caused by enemies poisoning him. Things like that. When that happened, it was impossible to reason with him. But he wasn't really dangerous. He had become quite frail by then." She let her voice trail off. Did Graham think she was drawing an analogy, comparing his behavior with her father's terminal dementia?

The faintest suggestion of a pained smile twisted his mouth. "You won't see me like that again, I promise. I thought I was over . . . her. Over it. And I guess, in a way, I am. It was just that being reminded hurt so damned bad." He put the beer down and leaned forward, cradling his forehead against the heels of his palms. "Oh, God, did that reminder hurt!"

"You loved her, didn't you?" Holly said cautiously, knowing he had to be encouraged to talk it out of his system.

"Loved her? Adored her! She wasn't just lovely to look at. She was lovely in spirit. Do you understand what I'm saying?" he begged, looking up. Holly nodded, waiting patiently. "She was like you. She knew when to listen, how to calm me down when I lost it. That special kind of touch. You've got it. You know what I mean."

"I'm trying to."

"And I don't care what kind of gossip you hear," he went on with ferocity. "I never touched her. No matter what Kyle thought. No matter what *anyone* thought. She was going to ask him for a divorce, but it wasn't because of . . . I swear I never laid a hand on her! We were friends, real friends, but not lovers. Not . . . we never got the chance," he finished, his sharp features pleading for Holly to believe him.

"Alanna. The woman in that portrait."

Graham nodded, dropping his head again. He turned the beer can around and around in his nervous hands.

In her mind's eye, Holly conjured the painting, the beautiful woman with green eyes. Alive, and so very much in love. In love with Russ Graham, this tortured artist.

He'd loved her, too. And he was the one who'd found her body, brutally torn by a dozen stab wounds. Holly imagined the poor woman's last, terrible moments as she saw death coming. As she realized she was going to die, and die horribly, mutilated, cut down by the searing pain of a knife striking her over and over and over . . .

"Here, don't!" Graham exclaimed, moving to the end of the couch, putting his arm around Holly's shoulders. She came back to reality and found she was shivering in empathic horror. "Damn me, anyway!" he said. "Shoveling my troubles onto you. Come on. Let's get out into some fresh air. I think we both need it."

He led her out of the studio. Cool lake air struck Holly's

face, drying the tears that had brimmed on her lashes. She inhaled greedily, clearing her head, forcing the hideous vision of Alanna's death out of her thoughts.

"Thank you." She forced a weak laugh. "I wanted to help you and end up being helped myself. Some clinician I am!"

His arm had dropped away from her shoulder, but he continued to stand close to her. His expression was solemn. "You did help me. That's the first time I've been able to talk about . . . about Alanna in a year. It's been a raw, open wound that never quite heals. I couldn't face the truth—that she was gone. I kept blanking it out, denying it."

"That's not wise," Holly told him. "You can't obliterate grief. You have to learn to cope with it, live with it—"

"Live with it?" Graham's manner turned wry. "Oh, I've lived with it. Lived with the whispers, too. Didn't they warn you about me? Aren't you afraid I'll end up stabbing you, like I'm supposed to have stabbed Alanna?"

A cold chill went down Holly's spine. "I . . . I don't—"

He didn't let her finish her protest, saying, "Oh, sure, the police let me go, after questioning me for hours and hours. And you can bet there are still plenty of people around here who are convinced I got away with murder. They think I tricked the police somehow, that it was really me who killed her," he snarled, outraged.

Holly held her tongue. Caring for her father had trained her well as a practical nurse and amateur psychologist. She'd learned far more than she'd ever wanted to about the dark places of the human mind. There were numerous scholarly studies pointing out that a man could indeed kill the thing he loved. Motives could vary. One was insane jealousy. Russ Graham made it clear that he'd loved Alanna deeply. If something had gone wrong, if she had decided not to divorce Kyle . . .

The hand which had gripped Holly's arm had been powerful—powerful enough to wield a knife and cut down a woman who, perhaps, had refused to become a man's lover.

Graham's hands were certainly strong enough. But . . . had he actually done the terrible deed?

"If the police let you go . . ." Holly said, speculating.

"They wanted to hold me as a likely suspect," Graham said with a snort. "And they've kept an eye on me ever since. Luckily, I had an air-tight alibi when the latest Butcher Knife Murder happened," he went on bitterly. Suddenly, he stared at Holly, worry in his eyes. "Look, when you're ready to return to Scorpio House, I'll walk you back. Okay?"

She was touched despite the tenseness of the situation. "I'm not afraid to be alone, Russ. For all practical purposes, I was alone for over a year, while my father was going through a long, slow dying. If anyone had broken into the house, he couldn't have protected me, or himself. But nothing happened. And nothing will happen to me now."

Graham shook his head, frowning. "That's not the same thing." He moved as if to place his hands on her shoulders, then thought better of the idea. Conflicting emotions chased over his sharp features.

Intuitively, Holly sensed the reason. He'd been hesitant to shake her hand at the party last night. She'd put that down to standoffishness. Maybe it wasn't that at all. Maybe he wasn't a "toucher." He might well associate touching with tenderness—and with loss of self-control. A man who'd been in military service might have been taught to suppress such feelings as that, in part as an act of self-preservation.

And yet, at this moment, he wanted to touch her, gently, but was holding back. Why?

"Not the same thing at all," Russ repeated. "Listen. I'd like to teach you how to handle a gun. Maybe get you one so you can defend yourself. I could handload it for you. A light enough load to discourage anyone who threatens you, but something you could fire without breaking your bones," and he reached out, his fingers making a circle around her wrist, not quite touching. His brows drew together. He was obviously planning a course of action. Then he looked sheepish and backpedaled. "That is, if you're willing. Perhaps . . . are you afraid of guns, Holly?"

"I don't know. A couple of my father's war buddies used to show off souvenir weapons they'd brought back from overseas. But that didn't affect me; I was usually busy elsewhere in the house, cooking or cleaning. I have no idea how I'd deal with guns up close. Mostly, I've seen them on television. And lately, strung all over the walls of your house," she finished slyly.

He smiled broadly. "Then would you let me teach you to shoot?"

"I think that might be . . . interesting."

"You pick a date. I promise I'll keep things simple. It's really easy, once you get the knack." Russ's face darkened, bleak with remembering. "God forgive me that I didn't teach Alanna how to protect herself. She might be alive today if I had."

"Oh, there you are, Pet," Bianca said in a tone of delighted discovery. She'd flung open Holly's bedroom door with a flourish and now posed on the threshold, gesturing dramatically. "I wondered where you'd disappeared to. You haven't forgotten about the picnic, have you?"

Mildly annoyed by the intrusion, Holly surreptitiously slid the papers in her hand under the coverlet. She bent to conceal her actions, pretending to tidy the bed and said innocently, "Is it time already?"

"Listen to her!" her sister exclaimed, laughing. "Don't tell me you haven't been counting the hours. I was with you when we shopped for just the right swimsuit, remember? And this past week Kyle and Russ have been tripping over each other, manufacturing excuses to drop by Scorpio House in order to see you. Purely by accident, I'm sure! And now she says 'time already?' "

Reddening, her annoyance deepening, Holly said, "I meant that this afternoon's gone by faster than I'd realized. I'll be ready in about half an hour."

Bianca ignored her, busy pawing through the closet, tossing a pair of shorts and a sleeveless blouse onto the bed. "These look great on you—white with a touch of golden yellow piping. It'll really make you sparkle, Pet. You'll have Kyle and Russ panting at your heels, not that they aren't doing that now. I always knew baby sister would be a belle if she put her mind to it."

"I'm not exactly a novice," Holly snapped. "I dated a lot at the university. The fact that the last year put me on the shelf didn't turn me into a nun . . ."

She might as well have been talking to herself. Bianca was selecting shoes to match the clothes, rummaging in dresser drawers, finding a scarf to add to the ensemble. All the while, she chattered. "This is going to be so much fun. Absolutely everybody's coming, even that writer who's been crashing at Russ's place. That's convinced Toby to go, too. Don't they make a dahling couple?" And with hammy exaggeration, she let a wrist go limp.

"Cut it out!" Holly said sharply enough to get her sister's attention. "Can't you be glad for them? Before Toby met Ivor Wilcox, I was sure he'd avoid this party like the plague. Something about . . . tell me: Did he and Kyle ever have a fight?"

Bianca's eyes widened. "Didn't you know? Oh, God! It wasn't a fight, but . . . as I understand it, when they first met, Toby had an awful crush on Kyle, or so Stephen told me. I . . . I guess Kyle sort of encouraged him. He probably thought it was a joke, being mistaken for . . . well, you know. Toby did all kinds of favors for Kyle, installing the latest electronic equipment in the Preis offices, going out of his way to be helpful."

"Kyle let him?" Holly said, frowning. "Leading Toby on?"

"Oh, of course not. It . . . it wasn't like that." The siblings exchanged stares. Holly recalled that this had happened long before Bianca had met Stephen Detloff or become acquainted with Dark Lake's social doings. It was just hearsay. Nevertheless, the implications were unpleasant.

Bianca shrugged, looking ill at ease. "Well, anyway, I gather Kyle finally told Toby to lay off, and in no uncertain terms. Since then . . ."

"Little wonder he didn't plan to attend the picnic," Holly said, then smiled and added, "but apparently Ivor's changed his mind."

"Oh, never mind about that. Now I'm holding you to your promise. Half an hour. Be ready!"

As the door closed behind her sister, Holly extracted the copy sheets from beneath the coverlet and spread them out. Glancing over them, her mind ran back over the past days. She'd been caught up in a whirlwind, it seemed. After serious thought, she'd accepted Stephen Detloff's offer. For over a week, Holly had been up to her elbows straightening out the jumble of Detloff's files. He had even insisted on advancing her part of her salary, giving her a measure of financial independence. When she and Bianca went shopping, Holly now could pay her own way and make her own selections for the first time in a very long while. Revenge had been sweet.

Working for Stephen was dizzying. The man moved in a total aura of astrological terms. Holly had listened closely, borrowed and studied his books, and tried to absorb the jargon as quickly as possible. No easy task. In the middle of a business conversation, Stephen was prone to lapse into references over "progressives," "radicals," "secondaries and primaries," and "the semi-arc school of casting." It was, if not Greek, at least a foreign and arcane language to Holly.

While struggling to learn his occupation's key points, she'd concentrated on the job she was assigned. Alphabetizing, categorizing, and organizing were her fortes, not transepts and occultations and occluded planets, whatever *those* were.

But during her general housecleaning and sorting, she'd come across certain files that had drawn her attention like a magnet. Feeling guilty, she'd made copies. The results now lay on her bed, for all the good they might do her.

If her dreams could be believed, her life was presently entangled with the astrological sign of Scorpio. Stephen had told her encouraging things about her natal Moon and Sun transit, pronouncing that her chart contained only "a few" malefics. Another time he referred cryptically to an angle of her tenth house and how Holly could well be clairvoyant.

She fervently hoped not! The last thing she wanted was for her dreams to be portents of coming events!

Charts and files and horoscopes. Stephen Detloff kept files not only on his paying clients but on everyone in his social circle as well, including Kyle Preis and Russ Graham. Each new acquaintance was grist for "Scorpio's" mill. He'd already worked out a horoscope for Ivor Wilcox and said his chart fitted well with Toby's; Stephen said they had "mutually strongly aspected Uranus and Venus and good positions in their seventh and eleventh houses."

And then there were those charts lying on her bed.

Russ Graham—a Taurean with a Scorpio Moon; at that bottom of the page Stephen noted: "Observe configuration of Uranus and the Sun—what a character!" How to interpret that comment? Or the heavily underlined "Uranus rising!" Holly hadn't wanted to ask for explanations, fearing she had already overstepped bounds by making copies of these pages.

Kyle Preis—Leo, and, again, a Scorpio Moon. Stephen had made an ominous notation: "Troubled fourth and a very bad twelfth house. And Sylvia is a double Capricorn! Most unfortunate!" There were even more unnerving scribblings below that annotation: "Saturn-Venus trine, not unexpected, naturally. Must try to help him overcome his difficulties—if that's possible. *Terrible* imbalance in western node."

Rereading all of that, Holly sighed. It was much too complicated for her very limited knowledge of the occult. But every day she became a bit more in awe of Stephen Detloff's legerdemain. His comments, far too often, carried a shivery ring of truth and struck home like a knife cutting through . . .

Holly gasped. Now why had she thought of *that* simile? She knew why, feeling cold. Her dream, all this talk about her being clairvoyant, and warnings regarding a menace from Scorpio entering her life. Plus, on the very day she'd arrived in Dark Lake she'd met two men whose astrological charts contained Scorpio Moons. Yet those two were as unalike as night and day.

Kyle, the social lion and publishing giant: handsome, athletic, and charming. But he was also a hag-ridden man, caught in a complex relationship web with his harpy mother, and still under the afflicted memories of his wife's murder.

Russ, an intense, talented artist haunted by his own involvement in Alanna's death. A man sometimes bitter, sometimes terrifying in his barely smothered rage.

Gooseflesh prickled on her arms. Holly shook off the mood and hid the horoscope pages in her vanity, then hurried to dress. She mustn't let doubts show during the picnic. But how to avoid that? During the past two weeks both Kyle and Russ had made no bones about their interest in her. Such attentions could be intoxicating, if she allowed herself to give into the temptation. She still had strong reservations about the entire situation. Both men, in very different ways, seemed to need her. Holly was keenly sensitive to that emotion; after all, she'd lived with it in Norris Falls. But Kyle and Russ weren't old men, weren't dying. They were young and vital.

And dangerous?

Stephen Detloff, too, carried the brand of Scorpio, didn't he? It was even the name he had adopted for himself and his residence!

Bah!

Constant speculation like this could lead to a total inability to function. She'd start seeing threats in every direction, if she kept this up!

Holly resolved to forget the charts and her dream. Bury it all! This was supposed to be a celebration of the glorious Fourth. She was going to a picnic attended by people who were fast becoming more than casual acquaintances. This evening was for *fun*.

The hell with gloomy thoughts and dire predictions!

But . . . it wasn't easy to push aside *all* the lingering worries.

Things went smoothly and trouble-free for a time. The Scorpio House "gang" dressed, assembled in the mansion's foyer, and sorted themselves out into their vehicles. After a short drive, they arrived at Kyle Preis's estate, a scant mile east of the Detloff property. The publisher had arranged a lavish picnic indeed for his friends. A huge dining canopy, colorful little dressing tents, and heavily laden buffet tables almost filled the wide lawn behind Kyle's palatial lakeside residence. Holly exchanged hellos with earlier arrivals and had almost forgotten her previous concerns when she heard her sister exclaim, "How absolutely fascinating! Ooh! It makes me shiver!"

Bianca, Maud, Cynthia Martin, and other picnic attendees clustered about Ivor Wilcox. The writer appeared to be holding an impromptu literary tea. Toby stood nearby, watching the show and smiling like a proud parent.

"You're really writing a book about the Butcher Knife murders?" Maud said in amazement.

"Sure am. I've already pitched it to my editor. She thinks it'll do great. Maybe even make the best seller lists."

Cynthia Martin looked dismayed, but her tone was polite as she asked, "And is that your specialty—true crime?"

"Oh yeah. I used to work the police beat for a Cleveland newspaper. Believe me, I saw plenty of stuff out there on the streets that'd curdle your milk."

Bianca, eager to assist, said brightly, "Then maybe you'll know how to get some inside information, interviewing local authorities and law enforcement and all that . . ."

Holly closed her eyes, counting to ten. She felt bedeviled. Was there no escaping reminders of those murders? Why couldn't people talk about something more cheerful? The cream of Dark Lake's society was gathered here on a beautiful late afternoon in July. A marvelous picnic layout awaited them for an evening of fine dining. This was a chance to swim, relax, and converse with friends. Servants had set up a stereo system near the buffet and soft music wafted over the scene. Despite all that, people congregated around Ivor Wilcox, listening avidly while he described the gory details of his project. From Holly's viewpoint, he was far too enthusiastic about the whole thing, like a kid with a new toy. It was true that he was new to Dark Lake, and therefore was probably able to regard the murders with some detachment, but still . . .

"Enjoying yourself, Princess?"

Startled out of her gloomy reverie, Holly looked up at Kyle Preis and returned his smile. Then she grimaced when she heard Wilcox warming further to his subject. Kyle nodded, sympathetic, and touched her arm lightly. She allowed him to lead her toward the buffet table and, mercifully, out of earshot of the "literary salon."

"I can't tell you how glad I am you finally decided to come over to my place," Kyle said with a grin. He picked up a couple of plates and offered one to her. As they began selecting from the array of goodies he went on, "I suppose I overdid it, hanging around Scorpio House and badgering you to visit. But whatever turned the trick, I'm delighted you're here." He paused and speared a deviled egg with a fork, saying, "I really don't bite, you know, except for yummies like these."

Holly laughed and added an egg to her own assortment of cold cuts and cheeses. "It's a magnificent spread, Kyle. And your house is beautiful." She glanced around and asked, "Is all of this yours?"

"As far as the hedge over there," he said, indicating the barrier with a sharp nod. "Mother's house is beyond." For a moment, his face lost all expression.

Alert to his shift in mood, Holly said quickly, "This grass looks like someone trimmed it with scissors. I've never seen such an immaculate lawn."

"That's what one pays high-priced gardeners for," Kyle gloated, cheerful again. "And general managers, etcetera." He swept an arm out, as if offering the property for her approval. Holly noticed that in the westering sunlight the row of colorful rented beach tents seemed to march down toward the lake like a string of jewels. Below them a wide pier reached out into the water. Fifty feet from the bank, an elaborate swimmers' float rode at anchor, bobbing gently on the waves.

Holly found every item on her plate was as savory as it was attractive. Kyle hired excellent caterers, as well as high-priced gardeners. As they finished eating, he began stroking the back of her hand with one finger, the same absent, mesmerizing touch he had used before. "I hope this won't be the last time you come here," he said, very earnestly.

"I'm sure it won't be."

His eyes gleamed. "Is that a promise? Then . . . could I put in a bid for a date? I know Stephen's keeping you busy now, but surely he lets you take some time off, hmm? We could drive into Chicago, take in a show, dinner, you know?"

"Not really," Holly said with a self-deprecating chuckle. "Remember, I've led a rather sheltered existence until recently."

"I remember. Stephen told me. Your father. That was wonderful of you. That kind of devotion. It's so rare these days . . . so very rare . . ."

Kyle's intensity took her aback, and the compliment made her redden. She tried to restore the lightness of the previous moment. "It does sound like fun. Yes, I think I'd like that. When?"

His grin was spotlight brilliant. "Just as soon as I can get everything set up properly. Got to get tickets, make reservations—"

"Looks like you cut me out, this time." At the sound of Russ Graham's deep voice, Kyle's hand tightened, momentarily painfully, on Holly's. Then, in the next breath, he had

116

released her and was offering that hand to the artist, greeting him warmly.

"Hey, Russ! Glad you could make it. What'd you think of the spread?"

"I haven't checked out the buffet yet, but I'm sure it'll be spectacular," Graham said, his attention on Holly. "Mm, I guess asking to cut in this early in the evening isn't quite protocol?"

"Nope! Not this time, buddy!" Kyle retorted, his smile wickedly triumphant. "You cut me out that night at the Martins. This is my turn. So shoo!"

Russ shrugged and said softly, "Best two falls out of three. See you later," and with that he walked away.

Uneasy, Holly said, "I don't want to be a bone of contention . . ."

"Naw! Nothing like that, Princess. We're good buddies again, ole Russ and me," Kyle told her. Smirking, he added, "But you know the best man always wins. Believe me, Russ is going to know he's been in a race before we're through." A salsa beat thumped from the portable stereo. Kyle stood and bowed and asked, "May I have this dance, milady?"

Holly confessed, "I'm afraid I'm out of practice. I haven't danced since college."

"Oh, ho! Then let me be the lucky guy who gets to give you a refresher course, mm?" He led her to an unoccupied spot among other couples on the makeshift but elaborate dance floor. Holly discovered Kyle was quite a good teacher and soon relaxed enough to enjoy herself thoroughly.

After a while, Russ Graham tapped Kyle's shoulder. The picnic's host blinked, caught off guard. With a rueful grin, he gave way with good grace. As Holly came into Graham's arms, she was torn between amusement and apprehension. Bone of contention indeed!

Both men were good dancers, but their styles were quite different. Kyle Preis was flamboyant, a bit of a showoff. Russ Graham moved smoothly, but his faintly ironic attitude gave the impression that he thought the whole activity was a trifle silly. Was he cutting in and dancing with Holly simply to show he could—and to test Kyle's position?

Holly found their attentions heady and flattering. Wary of acting foolishly, she continued to remind herself that she was, in effect, "fresh meat." Would these two men be as interested if another attractive young woman arrived at Dark Lake? Maybe. Or maybe not. She had enough ego, now, to tell herself she'd certainly give any newcomer plenty of competition. Or . . . how had Kyle put it? Show the newcomer she was in a real race.

As twilight descended, people began to drift toward the dressing tents. Holly followed the crowd. She and Bianca shared one of the little canvas rooms. They bumped elbows and hips as they changed into swimsuits. Bianca was giggling. "You're the belle of the picnic, Pet. I swear, I half expect Kyle and Russ to square off any minute. It's so cute, watching them fight over you."

"Don't be absurd. Come on: turn around and I'll hook your bra. Look, Bianca, don't push. Let things happen at their own pace, will you?"

"I just want to help," her sister protested, pouting. "Really! Which one do you like best?" Holly shook her head and started to spit a sharp rejoinder.

"Come on, you clowns! What's the matter? Bashful?"

Her planned retort stuck in Holly's throat. She and her sister eyed one another apprehensively, then Bianca peeked out of their tent and gasped. Jerking the flap shut, she said in a sharp whisper, "Good God! Sylvia and her flock of toadies are going skinny-dipping. She's way over the limit! Maud says she's beginning to think Sylvia's got a screw loose, and getting worse. Again."

"Again?" Holly asked, frowning in puzzlement.

Bianca nodded, sobering. "Maud said she hadn't seen Sylvia behaving this badly since Kyle was married to Alanna."

Holly made a disgusted noise and said, "Let's try to avoid her."

"Like trying to avoid a jumbo jet—a naked one." Bianca heaved a sigh. "Well, head back, shoulders erect, Pet. Onward."

For a while, people stood on the lawn, chatting, hesitating to go the rest of the way down to the lakeshore. Furtive glances and murmured conversations told Holly that everyone was appalled by Sylvia's exhibitionism. Sylvia, however, was oblivious to their opinions. She and her hangers-on cavorted across the grass, making toreador passes with beach towels. "Eat your hearts out, people!" the publisher crowed, flinging away her towel and striking a fashion model pose. Holly had to admit the woman had a good figure, but her face betrayed her age and a lot of living. Sylvia and her gaggle paraded toward the lake. They were an unattractive assortment of pendulous bellies and skinny, too-pale limbs. Squealing like a schoolgirl, Sylvia ran out on the pier and executed an expert dive.

Holly noticed Kyle standing a few yards away, rigid and staring, patently horrified by his mother's actions.

Suddenly, focus shifted away from Sylvia's horde. A shower of fireworks exploded over the lake. A chorus of "oohs" and "aahs" rose from the guests, and Holly heard faint shouts of delight coming from other residences scattered along the shore. Bianca pinched Holly's arm. "Aren't they gorgeous? Stephen arranges for it all. He has a boat anchored out there and hires men to put on this display every Fourth of July. What a lovely way to climax the picnic!"

"It sure is, and a lot prettier to look at than Sylvia."

"Enjoying the show, my dears?" Even wearing just swim trunks and shorn of his usual dramatic clothing, Stephen Detloff projected the image of a sorcerer. He walked with an odd grace, as though his feet didn't quite touch the ground. "Shall we try the waters?"

Bianca dipped a toe in and sucked in her breath, then said, "Oh, it's not bad at all. I thought it would be colder."

"It's a small lake, my love, and it's been a very warm season so far. Holly?" Stephen regarded her anxiously. "I never asked—can you swim?"

She smiled and said, "Not really, but I'm a very good floater. Don't worry. I don't intend to stray far from the shore." Her brother-in-law seemed relieved to hear that. He waited until Holly ventured waist-deep into the lake before he yielded to Bianca's teasing taunts and charged into the water after his wife. They reminded Holly of Titania being pursued by a lanky Oberon.

The water was just cool enough to feel good after a hot day. All around Holly people were beginning to play water games, splashing and shouting. Out in deeper water, near the float, picnickers laughed and dived and climbed back up on the raft to dive again.

Holly turned around slowly, letting the water bear her up. Chin deep, she looked toward the beach. Kyle walked slowly along the sand, occasionally kicking at it, struggling to control his anger over his mother's outrageous performance. At last, he ran into the water, stirring up waves and froth with the violence of his entry. Russ Graham stood near the end of the pier, watching Kyle for a moment. Then he dove into the lake, his slender frame limned by the glow of bursting fireworks and the tiki lights bordering the lawn.

Sighing, Holly leaned her head back, drew up her knees

and floated. Dark Lake's waters rocked her gently. Despite noisy pyrotechnics and swimmers' shouts, she felt serene. Thoughts, as well as her body, drifted. A childhood summer. Her parents and Bianca. Dim, happy images. Her father teaching her to float, telling her it was a skill that might save her life some day. He was a good man, kindly and sensitive, before disease destroyed his body and then his mind.

Holly stared up at fireworks crisscrossing the now-black sky, at the first stars twinkling into view overhead.

Her parents were gone, yet she was alive and happy, caught up in an interesting new life. It hardly seemed fair. The tears she had been unable to marshal at her father's funeral flowed now, sorrow mingling with happy childhood memories.

Sometimes the sounds of other swimmers seemed distant as Holly drifted. When those voices became too faint, she sculled with her hands, heading for the beach. She felt no fear, just a sense of caution. Her father had taught her never to panic in the water, saying she should simply draw her knees to her chest and she'd float to the surface.

Just the same, she knew she mustn't drift too far away from the others. After all, she had promised Stephen—

Strong arms closed around her, pulling her down.

As Holly went under, she had a split second to suck in a deep, desperate breath. She couldn't see anything in the blackness, only feel powerful hands and the terrible weight of water covering her head.

Struggling, struggling . . . unable to pull free . . .

Her father's words rang in her head: *Don't panic!*

She thrust away a frantic urge to scream.

Not underwater! She'd drown!

Holly continued to fight—uselessly. She was held tight in

121

a grip of iron, brutal, hard. One hand now atop her brow, pressing her deeper and deeper into the water.

Down . . .

Down . . .

Her lungs screamed for air. Darkness enfolded her like a massive, smothering blanket . . .

Consciousness, slipping away. Dreamy illusion, rushing upon her. A face, pressing against hers. Lips, hungry, demanding, bruising her own in a hurtful kiss . . .

And then . . . nothingness.

Chapter 7

Through a semi-conscious fog, Holly sensed that her face was once more in the open air. Reflexively, she sucked oxygen into tortured lungs and throat. Those inhalations made peculiar rattling sounds in her waterlogged ears.

She felt heavy, so very heavy, her entire body leaden. It was impossible to initiate any voluntary movement. Holly seemed to be a child again, lying in her own little bed, starting to drift off into dreamless sleep.

But a spark of defiance flared up within her mind, roaring, *No! You're not a child! You're a grown woman and you've nearly drowned! Wake up, dammit!*

And yet . . . hadn't she truly regressed to childhood? Holly realized, dimly, that she was being carried. A strong hand beneath her knees and an arm under her shoulders . . .

Daddy, carrying her into that little lake in Wisconsin? Carrying her gently, carefully, saying, "Don't worry, sweetheart. I won't let go of you."

No, please! Don't let go!

She tried to cling to that supporting presence, but lacked the strength.

Despite her waterlogged ears, Holly now began to hear other sounds. Laughter and splashing noises. Partyers, having fun. But very close by a masculine voice was shouting, "Stephen! Here she is! Hurry!"

Then she was no longer being cradled. A hard, gritty surface pressed into her back and the supportive hands were gone.

She wanted to cry out, to bring back that comfort. Instead, a paroxysm of coughing tore at her, and she gulped for air.

Voices all around her now. The pad-pad-pad of feet running across sand.

With enough effort to move a pyramid, Holly forced her eyes open, peering through wet eyelashes. Fireworks continued to dance overhead in the night sky, dazzling her still blurry sight.

Gradually, full consciousness returned. She found herself lying on the shore. Water lapped at her feet and ankles. Russ and Kyle knelt on either side of her. Both were dripping and laboring to catch their breath. Both turned and gestured urgently, repeating that call of, "Stephen! Hurry!" Fireworks and tiki lights lit both men's faces oddly and gave their features an eerie cast.

"Holly!" The astrologer was beside her now, dropping to his knees and looking horrified. "What happened? She said she'd stay close to shore . . ."

She wanted to explain and apologize for causing so much trouble. But all she could do was cough and splutter.

"Almost didn't hear her over the noise of those damned fireworks," Russ gasped, his shoulders heaving. "Barely realized somebody was in trouble. She was coming to the surface when Kyle and I found her . . ."

"Pet! Oh my God! Pet!" Bianca wailed and leaned over Holly, crying frantically. "Oh, God! Help her, please!" Holly wanted to reach out and touch her sister to reassure her, but she couldn't move her hands yet, and she couldn't stop coughing.

"I think she's breathing easier now," Kyle said. "She just needs to catch her breath. Give her a minute or two . . ."

"It's my fault," Stephen exclaimed, his tone anguished. "I promised to keep an eye on her. This is all my fault."

A final spasm of coughing racked Holly. Her throat and sinuses felt on fire. As she rolled onto her side, willing hands assisted her. A wave of embarrassment swept her as she spewed lake water and vomit onto the sand.

"It'll be all right, all right," Bianca murmured over and over. She'd grabbed a towel and was tenderly wiping Holly's face.

A babble of voices now surged around the little group by the water.

"Oh, it's Holly! What happened?"

"I *knew* we should hire a lifeguard . . ."

"That drop-off out there in the lake is so *sudden* . . .anybody could drown . . ."

"Bad vibrations, my dear, it has to be that . . . and the Moon phase . . ."

Holly's vision was clearing. She raised a shaking hand to push wet hair away from her eyes. Russ had found a beach towel and was wrapping it around her while Kyle tried to fend off curious onlookers. "She'll be okay, people. Just swallowed a lot of water. Stand back now, won't you? Give her some room."

Stephen wrapped a second, larger towel over Holly and said shakily, "Thank God! When I think of what might have . . ."

From somewhere out of Holly's range of vision a too-familiar, strident voice was braying, "That little idiot! Don't get so excited, everybody. She's just putting on a big drowning act. Oldest trick in the book, making you young studs feel all macho, saving her. She's really hooked you suckers—"

Kyle's face contorted with sudden rage. As Stephen, Bianca, and Russ were helping Holly sit up, Kyle leapt to his feet and shoved his way through the ring of spectators, confronting his mother. Holly blinked, trying to focus on the scene. Sylvia's platinum blonde tresses were sopping wet and plastered flat against her neck and shoulders; that bedraggled, fair mane clashed obscenely with the editor's dark body hair. She gaped at Kyle as he scooped up an abandoned beach towel and hurled it at her with such violence that she staggered under the impact. Sylvia clutched the rumpled terry to her naked belly, looking stunned.

"Goddammit! Go get some clothes on!" Kyle bellowed, his face red with anger. "You're disgusting. Quit trying to convince everyone that you're a giddy teenager who doesn't know any better. Either put something on, or leave. This is my property, not yours. Go somewhere else if you're going to play juvenile exhibitionist!"

"B . . . baby," Sylvia whimpered, holding out a pleading hand. Kyle's response was an ugly sneer. His mother slumped and looked every year of her age. Sobbing, she turned and fled through a break in the lawn's privacy hedge, seeking sanctuary in the adjacent mansion. For a moment, Holly almost pitied the woman.

Kyle ran his hands through his dripping hair and growled, "Dammit, dammit, dammit," as though that were a mantra. His expression was a war of conflicting emotions—anger battling remorse. Cursing, his words barely intelligible, he swung around and plunged into the lake, swimming furiously, plainly intent on going completely across the body of water before stopping.

Moving slowly, Holly got to her knees while Bianca cooed and fluttered and Stephen pleaded, "Please, don't exert yourself too soon . . ."

"Bring her up here," Maud ordered. Dark Lake's den mother was sitting near the party canopy. She patted an air mattress lying beside her chair. "Who in the hell wants to lie on wet sand? Come on, honey."

Solicitous hands—Bianca's, Stephen's, and Russ's—helped Holly to her feet and half carried her up the lawn. Their sympathy and concern comforted her even more warmly than the towels they'd wrapped around her. A comet's tail of other worried picnickers accompanied the group. By now, Holly had recovered sufficiently to feel pained chagrin: Look what she'd done! She'd ruined Kyle's party.

Or . . . had Sylvia ruined it?

As her supporters eased Holly onto the mattress, Maud made shooing motions and said, "Go on. Beat it. All of you. Give the kid a chance to pull herself together in peace. You heard me. Scram!"

Most of the crowd obeyed, drifting back toward the lake or finding good vantage points to watch the remainder of the fireworks. But Russ Graham and Holly's relatives lingered. Stephen asked intently, "Are you sure you're going to be all right? What *did* happen? You told me that you could float, were practically unsinkable . . ."

"I . . . I'm not sure . . . can't remember," she said. "Just need to . . . to catch my breath . . ."

His expression taut with concern, Stephen nodded and slowly turned away. As he did, Holly gazed after him with wary surmise. During the past week, she'd learned that her brother-in-law, despite his astrologer's reputation, wasn't infallible. Nor did he pretend to be. And yet, did he possess intuitive insight? Was it possible he had guessed the truth? His dark eyes locked on her, probing, almost demanding an answer.

What *was* the truth?

Indeed, what *had* happened out there in the water? Had it been some sort of sick prank turned bad? A mere ducking that nearly became lethal?

And those vivid impressions, just as she was losing consciousness. Had she dreamed that crushing encounter beneath the lake? Was it a fantasy spun by lack of oxygen? Had she imagined a hard body pressing against hers and voracious, hungry lips bruising her own?

If it *hadn't* been a dream . . .

A strange, perverted attempted murder, this. Someone sexually aroused? But instead of violating the victim, trying to kill her? As if only death could slake an all-consuming lust?

Russ and Kyle had saved her . . . or so it seemed. One of them ought to have seen her attacker, surely?

Unless . . . one of *them* was the attacker.

"Feeling okay, honey?" Maud asked anxiously.

Holly realized she'd gasped in reaction to the direction her thoughts were taking her. She nodded weakly. But those speculations wouldn't go away. If she hadn't been suffering from oxygen starvation, then something truly terrifying and strange had happened out there in the water. Her would-be killer could be anyone. Anyone strong enough to force her head under the water and keep it there. But then what? Had there been a last-minute change of heart? Perhaps other swimmers came too close during the incident and scared off Holly's attacker.

So many questions, and no answers.

Russ Graham swore he'd never touched Alanna. And, as Holly had observed, he certainly wasn't "a toucher." But was he a man who perversely abstained from "touching" only to vent his frustrated passions in a far more murderous fashion?

Kyle Preis, the charming, athletic, mercurial widower. Smooth and brimming with cultured manners. His explosion at Sylvia had shaken all who witnessed it. Holly had rarely seen such a rapid and shocking one-eighty turn in personality, except during her father's disease-caused mood shifts.

And Stephen, her charismatic, mysterious brother-in-law. It appeared that he was still on shore when the attack happened. However, appearances could be deceiving.

Holly heaved a sigh and crossed her arms over her eyes. She refused to think further about this tonight. Tomorrow, maybe she could cope, after her terror had faded somewhat. But not now . . .

People milled about on the lawn, taking a break from swimming, commenting on the fireworks. Watchdog Maud kept the others away from her, but Holly couldn't avoid hearing ongoing conversations—one, in particular.

"Six victims? I hadn't realized it was that many. They must catch this monster and put him away permanently." That was Jason Martin, speaking in his calm, eminently civilized tone.

"Sad to say, it is indeed six. I've checked the records very thoroughly," Ivor Wilcox confirmed. Holly could envision him ticking off points for his project on those thick, black fingers. "The Butcher Knife Murderer always kills a young woman, who is always alone. He always leaves the knife behind, and no prints. The police say the weapons are common discount store cutlery; no way to trace those, and he could buy them anywhere. One odd detail: Apparently none of the victims called for help, even though in several cases the evidence shows they were surprised or caught off guard."

"Is it possible that the women knew the killer?" Cynthia Martin suggested. "A boyfriend? Someone they wouldn't suspect, until it was too late."

"That's one theory," Wilcox said. "But, personally, I don't quite buy it."

"Could it have been a woman?" an unfamiliar voice asked.

"Huh uh. No way! Not unless it was an Amazon," Wilcox

told his audience. "I've seen the M.E.'s reports. This is one powerhouse of a murderer, one who overkills."

"A pervert?"

"No, not what you might think, though I'm interviewing a psychiatry honcho next week, so I'll have more data for a hypothesis after that. But a number of police experts already have gone out on a limb and said this killer has to be a psychotic. For one thing, there's a definite pattern," Wilcox said, his tone deepening. Unable to tune out what he was saying, Holly shivered. "The murders are committed no less than six and no more than eight weeks apart. It's as though this guy builds up a charge and then explodes. He always stabs his victims at least a dozen times before he disappears."

There were horrified murmurs as the author's audience digested what he'd told them. Someone ventured, "Don't the experts call that type sexually repressed?"

"Or maybe it has to do with phases of the Moon," another guest put in.

"That's an interesting angle," Wilcox said. "Suppose our world-famous astrologer here could work out some theoretical charts? How about it, Stephen?"

Holly heard a heavy sigh, then her brother-in-law saying patiently, "My dear Arien friend, astrology simply doesn't work that way. If you wish, given the pertinent data, I could work up material on the *victims* and their horoscopes. But it's impossible to cast a chart for a man I know nothing about."

"Hey! There you go, Ivor!" an interested listener exclaimed. "Let Stephen put together the victims' horoscopes and you'll have a different gimmick for your book—"

"Yeah! But can you afford his fee?" another said, and gales of appreciative laughter rang out.

When they dwindled, Bianca said with obvious disquiet, "Ivor, in what you've done so far, is there anything to tell us when *he* will strike again?" Holly lowered her arms and turned her head, watching the little group, her nerves jangling.

The black man frowned. "Well, I don't want to give anyone nightmares, but it's been over six weeks since the last murder. So one of these days . . ." Several women shuddered and Wilcox held up a hand. "Now don't get excited. You needn't worry, if your hearts are pure. The majority of his victims were . . . well . . . no better than they should have been, sorry to say. Prosties and bar hoppers looking for thrills and getting more than they bargained for . . . sort of asking for it—"

"Except for Alanna Preis." Russ Graham was standing at the outer edge of the little circle. Now he stared belligerently at his friend. "She didn't fit your theory."

Wilcox's expression and attitude shifted at once. "No, no she didn't. Sorry. Forgot about that lady, Russ. That's a big part of the mystery, too, that the pattern's been broken a few times."

The artist apparently accepted the apology. He nodded curtly and walked away, heading for the pier.

Holly mulled over what she'd heard. One could envision a prostitute taking a man to her apartment, where she felt safe, and being struck down there. Throughout history, there were certainly twisted male mentalities who took it upon themselves to rid the world of such women, as Jack the Ripper supposedly had. But what could explain Alanna Preis's murder? She wasn't a woman of the streets. The exact opposite, in fact. The portrait Holly had seen in Graham's studio wasn't that of an easy pickup. Alanna had obviously been class, a real lady, as Ivor Wilcox had called her. And yet that hadn't saved her from the Butcher Knife Murderer.

Did that mean Wilcox's theory was nonsense? Perhaps. Perhaps not.

Certainly, if Alanna Preis hadn't been safe, then no woman was safe.

Overdue for another murder, Wilcox said. The killer seemed to lie low, accumulating passion to the explosion point, then striking . . .

Passion becoming murderous frenzy.

Such as that possessing whoever had tried to drown Holly?

If that was—truly—what had happened. But . . . she couldn't be sure, could she?

She didn't put up much of an argument when Stephen manufactured a reason to leave the picnic fairly early. By that time Kyle was back from his cross-lake swim, and, with elegant courtesy, Stephen expressed his regrets to their host. Then the astrologer escorted Holly and Bianca to their dressing tent. Holly had recuperated enough to stand without assistance, though she was grateful for Bianca's help in hooking her bra and fastening her sandals.

On the drive back to the Detloff complex, Holly kept imagining a looming figure, surging out of dark water to seize her, or silhouetted in a doorway, knife in hand.

Every time she closed her eyes, a blood-red scorpion danced in her brain. She was tempted to snap imprecations at her brother-in-law for suggesting she was under some unspecified menace connected with the sign of Scorpio.

But Stephen Detloff wasn't to blame. He was no all-wise prophet, and he'd been at great pains to tell her so. Her reaction was like blaming an astronomer for discovering that the sun did not revolve around the earth. In Detloff's world-view, astrology, properly done, was the equivalent of pi—something that simply *was*, not his own creation. "Scorpio" wanted to help, but made no claims that he was an omniscient soothsayer. He warned Holly that her future might lay entirely in her hands.

When they reached the house, she brushed away offers to drive on to a twenty-four-hour clinic, insisting she was fine and fully recovered from her ordeal. Later, though, alone in her room, Holly did her best to wash away her fears with a hot shower. She toweled herself dry with rough, hard strokes, bringing blood rushing to her chilled skin. That didn't help much. In the end, she sought her bed like a frightened child, praying for sleep—*dreamless* sleep.

Chapter 8

"What do you think of her?"

It took Holly a moment to realize Kyle was referring to his foreign sports car. She was still sorting out impressions of his driving style and hadn't given much attention to the vehicle. When they'd left Scorpio House, she'd expected a gravel-throwing jackrabbit start. Instead, Kyle reined in the motorized power at his command and drove quite conservatively, at least on the back roads. Once they reached the expressway, he'd stepped on the gas, handling the car with great skill. "It's . . . I mean . . . *she's* terrific," Holly said. "The ride's so smooth, and yet it feels as if we're in the 500 race—"

"If we were, we might have a good chance of winning," Kyle finished for her, grinning widely. "She's a special custom job. There's plenty under that hood . . . *plenty.*"

Holly glanced at the speedometer and raised an eyebrow. "Do you ever get a speeding ticket?"

"Haven't for quite a while, though there was a time when my lead foot got me a few citations." He chuckled and went on, "But I've learned just how far and hard to push her—and where the traffic patrols are likely to be hiding." The publisher steered around a cluster of slower vehicles. "Too bad it's rainy, or I'd could put the top down."

Holly grimaced. "Well, I'm just as glad it's up, thanks. Otherwise, my hair and clothes would look like I'd been in a wind tunnel."

"You're right. Sorry. I should have thought of that myself.

134

I guess maybe it's lucky it is raining. Saved me from ruining things for you, eh?" Kyle eyed her briefly before returning his attention to traffic. "You're a darling to agree to leave so early, Princess. I hope I didn't rush you too much."

"Not at all." The slap-slap of windshield wipers underlined their conversation. Holly hoped the car wasn't prone to skidding; she still remembered that nerve-wracking incident in Russ's car, the last time she'd been on this expressway. Had that really happened only a few weeks ago? And it wasn't much over a week since she'd nearly drowned at the picnic. Things were moving at warp speed—just like Kyle's flashy car. "Really, I'm looking forward to a grand tour of Preis Publishing. Stephen's assigned me to proofread his new book. It'll be fascinating to see how it's put into finished form."

"Well, I'm not sure I can show you *that*," Kyle said, his tone apologetic. "We don't do our own printing and binding. But I *can* show you our editorial operation." He hesitated a moment, then asked, "Are you sure you don't mind stopping by the offices before we go to dinner?"

"Oh, not at all. I really would like to see where you spend your work days."

"Where I usually spend them," Kyle corrected her, looking smug. "That's the advantage in being boss. Ordinarily, if I wasn't calling the shots, I would have been stuck in town today. But as it turned out, the show tickets I got were for tonight, so I decided to play hooky and enjoy myself."

As the sports car ate up the miles, Holly marveled at the changes in her life. It seemed only yesterday she'd been trapped in Norris Falls as a small-town mouse, drudge, and practical nurse. Now she had a new job—working for her brother-in-law, a world-famous astrologer. She was rubbing elbows with all sorts of interesting people, including wealthy, dynamic Kyle Preis and moody, artistic Russ Graham.

For this evening on the town, Kyle had put aside the casual sports clothes he normally favored and was wearing a suit that must have cost four figures. His normal enthusiasm was overlaid with a touch of the debonair: appropriate, given his status as one of the nation's major publishers. His good looks and body-builder's physique made him look the part of a sophisticated, swinging bachelor. But Holly couldn't quite forget the facts casting a shadow over that glowing image of the man sitting by her side. Kyle Preis was a widower, and he was saddled with a harridan of a mother. Those details explained his occasional outburst of rage and the hint of smothered frustration in his character. Two women—one brutally murdered, the other very much alive and kicking—had left deep, indelible marks on the young publisher's psyche.

He was chattering about a boat race he'd attended recently, and as he spoke, Kyle reached out absently to caress Holly's hair. She bit back an urge to tell him to keep both hands on the wheel. So far, nothing in his driving caused alarm. And there was nothing lustful in his touch. It was more a fond gesture, a gentle expression of the pleasure he took in her presence.

A soft, buzzing noise interrupted Kyle's monologue. A dash light indicated an incoming mobile call. An adjacent cassette system began recording automatically. "Excuse me for a moment, Princess?" Holly nodded assent and gazed out the window while Kyle conducted a terse, no-nonsense business conversation with someone named Charlie. When he completed the call and the tape deck shut itself off, he said, "Sorry about that, Princess. No rest for the wicked."

"I understand. It's just like a movie: James Bond or a millionaire playboy, having all sorts of fancy electronic gadgets in their cars."

Kyle threw her one of his patented little-boy grins. "Just

like. It's a wonderful convenience, especially when I'm on the road between Dark Lake and downtown. I couldn't get anything done without my gadgets." He patted the panel containing the all-in-one speaker phone and recording device. "What's more, I installed it myself."

"You did? How clever!" Then Holly smiled slyly and said, "And you enjoy playing with it and showing it off, don't you?"

"Oh, yeah! Actually, there's not much to it, once you learn the tricks. I picked up most of the basics from Toby, of course. After that, I got to be drinking buddies with a guy who's pretty high up in the Internet octopus. You wouldn't believe the cute stunts you can pull, once you put all the stuff together." Kyle suddenly looked abashed, as though he feared he'd said more than he should.

Holly wondered if he thought she'd report his activities to some government agency. How absurd! "I think it's marvelous," she assured him. "It seems like magic. I mean, I have to concentrate very carefully, or I'll foul up using Stephen's copier half the time."

Kyle laughed and said, "Remind me to show you some shortcuts. I'd give the lessons lots more loving attention than you'd ever get from Toby, you bet!"

As they entered the fringes of the megalopolis, Kyle dealt expertly with ever-increasing streams of traffic. Now and then he swore when forced to dodge around a stalled car or a reckless driver. But all in all, Holly felt confidence in his driving, even amid this morass of vehicles.

Then they were arcing high over the city, lancing across the Skyway into the heart of Chicago, borne over a magic carpet. Night hid construction sites, grime, and decay, leaving an attractive glow of thousands of lights, shining like candles through the rain.

Kyle exited the Skyway and tooled along the well-lit

streets of a business district, finally turning in at a ramp. He stopped at an unmanned machine and inserted an ID card in its slot. After cogitating a few seconds, the robot tollbooth raised a grilled door and admitted them into a private parking garage.

"No attendant?" Holly asked.

"Not necessary. We're fully automated. Modern technology, at your service."

Kyle pulled into a reserved space beside another sports car bearing Sylvia Preis's vanity plates. As he gave Holly a hand out into the open air, her throat suddenly tightened with a burning sensation. "What *is* that?" she exclaimed, coughing.

"Smog fumes," Kyle explained, apologetic. "It's a weird phenomenon. Bothers me, too, sometimes. The rain does it—brings all the pollution down to street level. Things will be better indoors. Come on." He touched her elbow and guided her to an elevator.

They shot skyward at a speed which made Holly's stomach flip-flop. The lift sighed to a stop at the twelfth floor and doors opened onto an expensively-decorated foyer. That entryway connected to an immense office area labyrinthed into glass-walled cubicles and carpeted corridors. To Holly's surprise, at least half of the cubicles were occupied.

"Doesn't anybody go home after work?" she said, puzzled.

"Not if we want to beat the competition," Kyle replied with a grin. "We use a lot of flex time here, and most of our editors set their own schedules. If there's a deadline pressing, they'll hammer as long as it takes. I do the same. It's just that right now I'm sort of between projects . . ."

Printers chattered, phones chirped, keyboards clicked. Kyle moved along the main corridor, now and then exchanging greetings with his employees. His hand remained on Holly's elbow, his touch light but possessive.

She noticed that some of the male editors eyed her speculatively, and some of the younger women glared at her. With envy?

"Ah, there you are, kiddies." Sylvia emerged from the main office at the far end of the corridor. She wore an auburn wig so stiff with spray Holly suspected she'd cut her finger if she dared touch the thing. In a departure from past sartorial exhibitions, the publisher was dressed in a modest navy-colored suit, though it *was* cut a size too small.

There was a noticeable difference in her behavior as well; Sylvia's voice was softer than usual and her manner far less brassy. Holly wondered if that was because this was Sylvia's personal domain, a place where she felt completely at ease. Perhaps there was no need for her to play dominance games here. "I thought you'd forgotten about that Hastings manuscript, darling."

"Not a chance," Kyle said, and gave his mother a polite peck on the cheek. He turned to Holly. "Will you excuse me for just a minute? I have to check out some figures in my office. Be right back."

The two women were left alone in the corridor, eyeing each other warily. Then, to Holly's surprise, Sylvia began oozing sweet reasonableness. "I hear you kids are off to do the town. I hope Kyle's made reservations at Tiampi's. They have the most marvelous seafood you'll ever sink a tooth into. Tell the maitre'd I sent you, will you, dear?"

Seafood ranked close to the bottom on Holly's list of favorite foods, but she forced a smile and a nod of gratitude for the suggestion.

The publisher laid a red-clawed hand on her arm and said, "I set him up with tickets for that new musical, you know. Fringe benefit of this business—free passes like rain from heaven."

"That must be very nice . . ."

"Let me tell you something, dear," Sylvia whispered, leaning close. "I am *so* glad Kyle's dating *you*. I tell you, I was worried sick when he was going on nothing but trashy one-night stands. You know? And after the hell he went through last year . . ." Her voice dropped into a whiskey-contralto range. "I wouldn't tell this to another soul, and especially not to Kyle, poor boy. But it was a blessing from heaven when that little tramp Alanna got what was coming to her. Somebody sure did my boy a favor, believe me. She was cheating on him, you know."

Stunned, Holly stood mute. The situation made her want to squirm free of Sylvia's grip and run out into the comparative cleanliness of Chicago's smoggy, rain-soaked night.

Sylvia took her silence for agreement and rattled on, "He's such a sweetheart, and he deserved *so* much better than Alanna. I *tried* to talk him out of it, God knows, but you know how impulsive that boy can be. Kicks up his heels, just like a wild colt. Takes after his father. Never could tell Dan what was good for him, either. But now with *you,* dearie, I'm feeling confident that everything's going to work out the way it should."

Where were the daggery, vicious glares Holly had endured previously? This saccharine, cloying pose didn't fit the Sylvia Preis Holly had come to know and heartily dislike. And yet . . . in a way, the change made a kind of crazy sense. The woman obviously hadn't approved of Kyle's marriage. Sylvia probably had done everything in her power to prevent its taking place. And afterward she must have tried hard to drive a wedge between the couple. By her own admission, she was delighted when Alanna had been murdered. But Alanna's death hadn't brought Kyle back fully under his mother's control. If Sylvia was Jocasta, then her Oedipus was refusing to play his part. At the picnic, her performance had been so grotesque that Kyle had exploded, publicly shaming her.

Apparently Sylvia had decided on a different plan of action: If you can't beat 'em, join 'em. Perhaps she hoped to win her way back into Kyle's good graces by being friendly with his latest interest.

Or . . . was this simply another devious, nasty tactic? Holly remained very much on guard. She suspected that just beneath Sylvia's gushing surface, there was seething jealousy and hatred enough to consume any younger rival, if the publisher dared turn loose her wrath.

"Holly? Care to come in and see how the great man operates?" Kyle had poked his head out of the office to the right and beckoned Holly to join him. Grateful to escape Sylvia's clutches, she hurried inside.

"You kids have a good time! Hear?" Sylvia called after them, almost wistfully, before returning to her own office.

As Holly slipped into Kyle's sanctum, he was cueing a large computer setup, one closely resembling Stephen's system. "Just a few minutes longer, Princess," Kyle promised. "After all that time on the phone, I couldn't get hold of Hastings, so I'm setting a tape message to catch him later."

"This looks like the equipment at Scorpio House."

"It should. They're both Toby's babies. I'll give him that: He's a techie genius. If only he . . ." Kyle trailed off, reddening slightly. "Well, maybe he's happy now, with that crime-story author."

"Toby's been whistling while he works, lately," Holly said, hoping to shunt the conversation in another direction.

"Where did he and Wilcox meet, anyway?" he asked casually.

"At Russ's."

"Oh," Kyle said, his expression unreadable. "Service

buddy? What were they, Navy SEALs, something macho and deadly like that?"

"I don't really know. He's never mentioned his military background. But Russ said Ivor was a college chum, so I assume that's where they first made contact."

Kyle nodded, accepting her words without comment. He finished his work at the computer center and went to his desk. There he scribbled a message on a steno pad, then flipped the lock opening the door of a smaller, adjoining office. As he tossed the pad onto a desk in there, he smirked and said, "That'll make my secretary's day tomorrow. Well, I guess that's it," he decided, glancing around the room. "Come on. Let's use the other door. Don't know why I didn't come in that way. Yes, I *do* know; I wanted to show you off to all the watercooler Joes out there and make 'em eat their hearts out."

He led the way to a second door accessing directly from his office to a back hall. Holly wondered aloud, "Shouldn't we say good-bye to your mother?"

"No." Curt and guarded. Kyle went on with an effort at lightness, "No need to report in every time I'm on a date. I'm a big boy now."

They left the building via empty corridors, and used a different elevator. When Kyle drove out of the parking garage he accelerated so rapidly Holly feared he would crash through the protective grille at the exit. At the last moment, he hit the brake and methodically ran through the ID system at the automated booth. Holly bit her lip, resolving not to mention Sylvia again for the balance of the evening.

She carefully stuck to safe topics throughout dinner in a lavish restaurant, often employing what Bianca called her "secret smile." Apparently it was an effective move; Kyle seemed fascinated—or more correctly, believed that she thought whatever *he* said was fascinating.

"How do you like it?" he asked, indicating her plate.

"Mm! It's delicious. I'll have to bone up on my French so I can order it if I'm ever here again."

His hand reached across the table and closed over her free one, his thumb busy on the backs of her fingers. "Unnecessary. Any time your appetite demands, I'll bring you here. Guaranteed. Or anywhere else your heart desires." In the restaurant's muted lighting, his gaze was nearly as intense as Russ Graham's. There was also a tacit pleading in his manner, as if he were begging for love and understanding. "You . . . don't take this the wrong way, Holly . . . but you remind me of Alanna. Do you mind me saying that?"

Whether she did or not, she knew what response she must make. "Not at all. I'm flattered. From all I've been told, she was a lovely person. Everyone says she was the sweetest lady alive. I can't pretend to compare myself to her, but if you—"

"It's not that you look like her," Kyle said. "You're shorter, and your hair's a lighter color, and your eyes . . ."

"Aren't green, just a lackluster grey." Holly was afraid he was going to become maudlin about his dead wife, and wanted to keep things on a lighter level. She failed.

"Who told you Alanna had green eyes?" he demanded, suddenly very alert.

"I . . . uh . . . I guess it was Maud," Holly lied. It didn't seem wise to mention the portrait in Russ Graham's studio.

"Oh. Yeah. Maud tells everybody everything. Don't get me wrong; I love that gal, each inch and pound, but . . . well, sometimes I'd prefer some privacy, to have things belong only to me. Does that . . . does that make me too possessive?"

"I . . . I'm not sure," Holly murmured, lying again. Had Alanna been a beautiful toy for Kyle's amusement, custom-made for him to adore and possess? If so, he might have resented fiercely any intrusion on his private paradise, such as rumors that Alanna had a lover—Russ.

"We were going to pull up stakes, just the two of us," Kyle said, staring into space, his thumb continuing to caress Holly's hand. "It was our secret. Alanna told me I ought to strike out on my own, maybe start my own branch publishing house. Break clean. Get away from all that financial crisis left over from Dad's . . ." He stopped, his expression bleak, then brightened as he went on, "California, maybe. I like the Coast. Always have. Alanna said if we went there . . ."

Mentally, he was thousands of miles away, in a never-to-be dreamworld out west, and a year or more in his past. Kyle and Alanna, getting away, escaping from bitter memories of his father's suicide, questionable financial dealings, and, most of all, cutting that umbilical cord binding him to Sylvia.

"I'm a big boy now."

But was he, really? Couldn't he have broken away from his filial shackles long ago, if he truly wished to be free? His savage outburst at the picnic had shocked his guests precisely because it was so totally unexpected. Bianca had said as much later, telling Holly that Kyle had always put up with Sylvia's antics previously, no matter how gross they had been. It was only at the picnic, when his mother had made the crack about Holly, that Kyle had erupted like a long-dormant volcano.

Or . . . had that simply been the only such incident his friends and acquaintances had witnessed? Had Alanna, too, been caught in the middle of that maelstrom, an ever-raging love-hate war between mother and son? Had there been other eruptions, when the three were behind closed doors in a Dark Lake mansion, hidden from outsiders' eyes?

Slowly, Kyle came back to the present. He lifted Holly's hand and kissed it, very gently. "You listen to me. Really listen, just like Alanna did. Thank you."

Holly was deeply moved, but hastened to steer conversation to another topic. She asked about the show tickets, paid close attention while he waxed enthusiastic about the hit musical. As he swept back into that upbeat, boyish side of his personality, she began to relax.

A delightful several hours followed. They had box seats for an extravaganza of fabulous music delivered by world-renowned actors. When the lights went up at intermission, Holly discovered she and Kyle were surrounded by celebrities, the elite of Chicago's society. During cocktails in the lounge, Kyle introduced her to a bewildering stream of his acquaintances from the entertainment industry, sports, and business. Gradually, she became aware that she was an ornament, almost a trophy. Kyle's male friends teased him for "hogging all the good-looking women." One comic star who was famous for his acid tongue cracked, "He finds 'em everywhere, even in Dark Lake. Now where the hell is Dark Lake? Sounds like something from a soap opera. Hey, Kyle, baby, any more at home like this cutie?"

Kyle, his hand on Holly's elbow as he led her back toward their box, called over his shoulder, "Just one. A gorgeous sister. But you're too late: Stephen Detloff got her."

The comedian shouted a jovial vulgarity after them.

It was in the early hours of Friday morning that the fairy tale evening finally began winding down. The sports car's tires hummed on the rain-slick pavement as Kyle drove east toward Dark Lake. Holly, pretending drowsiness, reflected on all that had taken place. Touring Preis Publishing, dining at an elegant restaurant, attending the theatre, a late-hours club crawl, dancing to headline bands . . .

She risked a sidelong glance at Kyle. He was visibly enjoying himself, expertly handling the minutely-shifting steering wheel, exulting in his control over the powerful machine. His full, sensuous lips were slightly parted over perfect teeth in a happy, reminiscent smile. Obviously, he wasn't thinking of Alanna any more, or of establishing his not-quite-independence from Sylvia. Was he basking in the pleasure of an evening spent in Holly's company? Or was he relishing memories of envious men and jealous women? Envious and jealous of his new property.

Was that what he thought she was? Property? And had Alanna been . . . property? If so, had the dead woman accepted the idea wholeheartedly? Russ said Alanna loved *him*, and was going to ask Kyle for a divorce. Had she? Had she been torn between her wedding vows and a growing love for the artist? And had Alanna proposed moving to California as a last-ditch attempt to save her marriage? Perhaps she hoped to escape Sylvia's malevolent influence as much as Kyle did. And perhaps she wanted, also, to escape an ever-increasing danger of falling hopelessly in love with Russ.

Property. Did Holly want to be Kyle Preis's property? Not really. She wasn't inclined to be *anyone's* property.

Considering the situation from another angle, she asked herself if she wanted to take Alanna's place. That was an interesting question. There were certainly positives associated with that position—wealth, a handsome man's adoration . . .

But taking Alanna's place might also entail repeating that young woman's tragedy, dying, as Alanna had died, bloodily and horribly.

No, better not go *there*. Not until she'd had a chance to examine the pros and cons of this from every possible angle and eliminate any potential danger!

They left the expressway and sped through the darkness along state and county roads, then onto a familiar two-lane blacktop. They were entering Dark Lake now.

Time for Cinderella to turn in her remaining glass slipper.

Holly giggled and Kyle looked over at her quizzically. The glow from green dash lights created a sinister glow across his features and fair hair. "What's funny?" he asked.

"I just thought of myself as Cinderella, and had a weird mental picture of your car turning into a pumpkin."

He laughed with her. "Afraid it's a trifle late to consider that, Princess. It's way past midnight." Holly squinted at her watch and gasped, and he laughed harder. "Forget it. I'm sure Stephen won't mind you playing hooky tomorrow—uh, I mean, the rest of today. Get your beauty sleep. Keep yourself pretty for me, huh?"

As they rolled up the drive to Scorpio House, Holly debated the protocols of her next move. Should she invite Kyle in? She decided the very fact of her indecision was a tip-off to her true feelings. No commitments or steps she couldn't retrace. Not yet.

The evening—night—ought to end on a light, non-intense note.

Kyle helped her from the car and held her elbow as they ran through the rain to the portico. Out of the storm, but still feeling the mist, they stood before the great double doors. Kyle's hand caressed Holly's throat and tugged gently at her hair. "Princess, I could push my luck all kinds of ways tonight. But I don't think I will. I . . . I want this to be like . . . like it was with Alanna. Do you understand?"

Relief swept Holly. So, he *didn't* regard her as just a one-night stand, part of a string Sylvia had referred to. Kyle bent his head and kissed her, sweetly, not pressing. He seemed to have himself on a tight leash, protecting his property-to-be.

147

Mustn't paw or let loose his lust, or he might damage the merchandise.

When he finally withdrew, his expression was a bit fatuous, as if he were proud of himself for being the utter gentleman. "Look, I've got to participate in a charity golf tournament this weekend, starting tomorrow—uh, I mean today. So I won't get a chance to see you. Can I call you Monday?"

"Of course. I'll be at work in Stephen's office."

Kyle grinned in anticipation and waited while she slipped inside Scorpio House.

She heard the roar of his car tearing down the drive and half expected the sound of a crash, but there was none.

"I came to put out the cat."

Holly whirled, startled. Toby Carmichael, in robe and pajamas, got up from a chair near the alcove under the stairs. Obviously, he had been waiting for her arrival.

"Oh, Toby. I'm so sorry to have kept you up this late."

He went to the door and bolted it, then set a series of burglar alarm switches.

"That's what I get paid for," he said, very short. Then his manner softened as he studied her. "Did you have a good time?"

"Very nice. Dinner and a show and dancing. I met dozens of celebrities. Oh, and we went to Preis Enterprises. I saw your computers there."

"Did you?" A darkness crossed the little man's elfin face. "It's a damned good system. I hope Kyle's keeping it properly maintained." Toby paused, regarding her still more closely, then said, "Holly, forgive me if I'm getting out of line, but are you falling in love with him?"

Holly smiled weakly. "I . . . I'm not sure. It's too early to tell."

"Is it?" He spoke with the fatalistic tone of someone who regretted his own impulsiveness in affairs of the heart. "Alanna fell for him like a ton of bricks, the moment she met him. I thought all women did." Toby hesitated, then plunged ahead. "Could I give you some advice? Not that I think you need it; the better I get to know you, the sharper you get. But . . . take your time, will you? Just take your time. I think that was Alanna's trouble. She didn't take her time, got swept off her feet, and then it was too late." He shook his head sorrowfully. "Oh, hell! Forget I said anything. Good night." With that, he disappeared through the door in the alcove.

Holly made her way upstairs, moving slowly, thinking hard. Cinderella home from the ball, and kissed good night on the doorstep by Prince Charming. Prince Charming with a dead wife—dead in the most horrible fashion imaginable.

So Alanna had fallen head over heels the moment she met Kyle. Then what happened? Had Kyle's possessiveness overwhelmed her? Being paraded about like an expensive jewel might wear very thin. Eventually, that arrangement could prove suffocating to the sunniest nature.

And then Alanna found herself falling in love with Russ.

Half asleep, Holly undressed and put her Cinderella gown on a hanger. She kicked off the stylish but uncomfortable heels and got ready for bed. For some reason, her eyes were drawn to the *Aquarius* painting. A dancing figure on a calm, blue background. How she longed for such calmness!

The picture blurred, became Alanna's portrait. A beautiful young woman with dark hair and green eyes.

Two men had loved her, and now Alanna was dead.

And both men had said almost exactly the same thing: Holly reminded them of Alanna. Not physically. But something in her personality and manner echoed what both men found desirable in Alanna. If only Russ had remarked on that, she could have dismissed it as mere wishful thinking. If only Kyle had done so, Holly would have put it down as a line to be used on the new girl in Dark Lake.

But both of them!

Both had loved a woman, and she'd died.

According to Stephen Detloff, Holly was living under an unspecified menace, one linked to Scorpio House. Bianca had laid the groundwork for Holly's uneasiness even before her sister had met the astrologer.

Had Alanna Preis lived under such a threat, too? Was Holly now reliving her life, as she might relive Alanna's tragedy?

Nonsense! It was all nonsense! It must be!

Teeth chattering, she crept into bed, dragging the sheets close about her throat, burying her head in the pillows. She would *not* think of this stuff, nor would she dream!

But as she drifted off, a demonic, impish cackling rang in her subconscious.

You will dream and know terror. And the worst will be that you won't be able to tell if your fear is caused by suggestion, superstition, or if, indeed, you will soon be staring sudden death in the face.

Chapter 9

"No, it won't work if you simply pull the trigger. First, you have to pull back the hammer," Russ explained. His hands closed over Holly's, guiding hers. "*Now* it's cocked, so be careful not to point it at anything you don't want to hit. Line up the sights on the bull's-eye."

She frowned, listening intently to be sure she didn't miss any nuance of his instructions. That wasn't easy; because he'd insisted she wear a set of padded headgear like his own, and the things muffled his voice. "Will it recoil much?" she asked anxiously.

"I put in very light handloads, but it'll buck, sure. And the sound will be louder than you expect, even with those hearing protectors."

They stood at the waist-high bench, south of the artist's house. The blowout's side loomed several yards ahead of them. Russ had tacked a target to a wooden backstop built against the wall's face. That bull's-eye seemed to challenge Holly. She knew she was revealing her ignorance of this sport with every move, yet was determined to be a good student. Too many terrifying dreams, plus Ivor Wilcox's daily gruesome updates on his book-in-progress, had made shooting lessons seem like a very sensible idea. When Russ called this Sunday to repeat his invitation, she'd jumped at the offer. Now, her arms shaking from the unaccustomed effort of holding the heavy weapon, she was having second thoughts.

"Do you really think I can do this?" she wondered aloud.

Initially, she'd envisioned herself as an Amazon sharpshooter and butt-kicker, capably fighting off would-be rapists and murderers. Reality, underlined by the revolver's weight, swept away those delusions.

"Maybe not with *this* gun," Russ said, "but at least you'll get a taste of target shooting. If you decide to go on, I'll take you to my favorite sporting goods shop and we'll pick out a smaller model handgun for you. Okay?" She nodded and bit her lip. Russ steadied her trembling arms and hands. "When you're ready to fire, take a breath and hold it, then pull the trigger."

"I thought I was supposed to squeeze it."

"You heard that on TV, didn't you? Forget it. This isn't a shoot-'em-up cop show," the artist said with a contemptuous snort. "And that gun doesn't have a hair trigger. Just pull it— *smoothly*. Don't jerk it."

She braced herself and forced her extended arms to quit wobbling for a few seconds. Clutching the pistol grips with both hands, Holly managed to steady the sights on the target, inhaled, held her breath, and pulled the trigger. A roar shattered the quiet afternoon. The gun arced upward until she held the weapon pointing almost directly over her head.

"That wasn't so bad, was it?" Russ said, his pale eyes twinkling. He took the gun from her stinging hands and carefully laid the pistol on the bench rest. Using a pair of field glasses, he checked the target. "A little high and to the right. Take a look."

"Hey! I actually hit it, didn't I?" she exclaimed in happy surprise. "I didn't think I was even close to the paper."

Russ looked amused. "Well, you were. Now try it again."

With some trepidation, she obeyed. Even though she was now prepared for the recoil and noise, she staggered a trifle

each time the gun fired. Russ encouraged her, keeping up a running commentary on her progress. "Better, but you're still hitting slightly high and right. When you get your own gun, I'll sure have fun adjusting its sights for you. Try aiming a bit left and down."

Even with the hearing protectors, Holly's eardrums protested, but she continued to shoot—until she cocked the hammer and pulled the trigger, and nothing happened.

Chuckling, Russ took the gun. "Five's all you get. Here, take a look at your last shot," he said, handing her the glasses.

To her delight, she saw a ragged hole at the upper right edge of the bull's-eye. "I nailed it!" she cried.

"Definitely. Not bad at all, for a first lesson. With a lighter gun and properly adjusted sights, you ought to be a pretty fair target shooter."

Holly watched him reloading the revolver and said, "My father used to have a gun like that. Sort of. I remember seeing him clean it when I was younger. We had to sell it later on, to pay medical bills."

"That's rough. Do you remember the make and model?" She shook her head, and he went on, "I can just imagine how much that pained him, having to give it up."

"He had to give a lot of things up." Russ eyed her thoughtfully as she went on, "I spent a lot of time suffering, second person, for him, while he got sicker and weaker, and became helpless. Then his mind started to go." Holly paused and stared into nothing for a long moment. "That sort of thing can make one awfully bitter."

"But you didn't let that happen, did you?" Russ's expression was admiring at first, then gradually changed to a taut grimness. "Frankly, you've just described my own private version of hell."

"I'm sure it was hell for him, too. He was a good man . . . a

good man. I went through my own kind of hell, seeing him dying and going mad by inches."

"Here." Graham offered her the reloaded gun, giving her a noisy distraction to chase away bad memories.

Holly's first two shots were fairly accurate. The last three were not. "It's getting hard to hold it steady. I guess the gun's just too heavy for me. Besides, my ears are really complaining, despite these." She pulled off the hearing protectors and shook her hair free.

"They'd be ringing worse, if you weren't wearing those. Believe it or not, you were firing extra light ammo; I put together a batch of special loads for you." Russ opened a second box of cartridges and reloaded the gun, advising her, "You'd better put the hearing protectors back on. This is the real stuff, what I normally use, in case of burglars or whatever."

Holly nodded and said, "I understand. You have some extremely valuable artwork in your studio. That would certainly tempt thieves."

He laughed. "Not nearly as much as my guns would. It's a vicious circle: You own a gun to guard against thieves who want to steal your guns." He waited until Holly had fitted the hearing protector back over her ears, and then—as she thought of it—addressed the target. There was elegance in his stance. He took the revolver in one hand, turned his right shoulder toward the backstop, raised the weapon, and sighted on a second, as yet unmarked paper target. With a smooth deliberation speaking of long practice, he cocked the gun and fired.

Holly had been mistaken. Her lesson hadn't been noisy at all. In rapid succession, five cracks of thunder exploded from the gun. Russ paused a mere fraction of a second between shots, deftly operating the revolver's action. The artist's

strength awed her; she remembered what an effort it had been for her to hold that bucking pistol steady with *both* hands.

Echoes still seemed to ring while she examined the target with the field glasses. "I . . . I think you obliterated the center of the bull's-eye."

"Actually, that target's too large for this short a range," he said, shrugging, but he obviously was pleased with her report. As he extracted empty shell casings Russ added, "I just needed to make sure I wasn't getting rusty. You want to do any more shooting? Then let's knock off and give your ears a rest, and get in out of this hot sun."

As they trudged through the sand toward his studio Holly said, "I thought Toby and Ivor might be here this afternoon. But I guess they went somewhere with Bianca and Maud and Cynthia."

"Yeah, some kind of literary tea," Russ muttered. "The women showed up here about one, in that tank of Maud's. Said they'd probably be gone most of the day. Ivor's become the social lion of Dark Lake. And you're the lioness," he finished, regarding Holly with a look that made her blush.

"Hardly," she protested. "I'm not a well known author like Ivor, but if I were, I certainly wouldn't pick a topic like . . . like . . ."

"The Butcher Knife murders? I didn't know Ivor was going to get so damned wrapped up in that case when I let him move in here. But there's no stopping him now. Once he gets rolling on a project, he's like a juggernaut. He's already put together a huge pile of research. Some of it might even interest the police. He dug into a wide variety of sources, including some the cops probably didn't have the legal right to investigate. I'm beginning to think he really *will* make the best-seller lists with this one. It's certainly sensational enough to attract the morbidly curious . . ." Russ winced, as if thinking of Alanna's death. He shook his head and changed the subject. "I wasn't sure if you'd accept my invitation today. Figured maybe you'd be out on the town again with Kyle."

Holly studied him sidelong, wondering if that was a feeler of some sort. Was there a tinge of jealousy in his query? "Oh? How did you know about our date?"

He held open the screen door for her and let it bang shut behind them. Russ carefully opened the gun's cylinder and placed it on the coffee table before he answered. "I called Toby." His tone revealed nothing but bare information.

"Mm. Of course. Well, anyway, Kyle's otherwise occupied—some golf tournament that's supposed to last all weekend."

Russ grunted, sat down, opened a kit, and began to clean the pistol. Plainly, that was a task he could have done in his sleep. He pointedly avoided looking at Holly as he said, "I'm a long way from being in Kyle's class in the entertainment department. I suppose he took you to a hit show and a fancy restaurant, right? Best I could offer is an occasional meal at Pietro's or an art fair or rock concert, or a shooting match."

"Those all sound like fun," Holly said, sitting beside him. He grunted again, his expression sour. She went on warily, "Since I started working for Stephen, I've asked him hundreds of questions about astrology. Did you know he has horoscopes on file for everyone he knows? Including you. He says you have Uranus rising in your chart. When I asked him what *that* meant he told me such people, among other things, are likely to be gruff, abrupt, and of uncertain temperament. I don't believe in any of it, of course, but I must say that particular comment seemed dead on target."

Russ turned to stare at her. Then a reluctant grin split his lean features. "Of uncertain temperament, am I? And here all my friends tell me I've got a perfectly even temperament—always bad."

"No, it isn't," Holly said quickly. "But you *do* keep your better side awfully well hidden a good share of the time."

He rubbed a cleaning rag over the re-assembled pistol and replied, "Maybe I'm living too much in the past, nowadays. I didn't used to be this way, not when Alanna . . ." He wadded up the rag and hurled it toward a trash basket. In contrast, his movements with the gun were slow and careful—fitting it snugly into a holster before he laid it aside on the table. "Did Stephen also tell you that Uranus has something to do with notorious murderers? Just what, I'm not sure. So does the sign of Scorpio, I gather. And he said, a long time ago, that I also had a Moon in Scorpio, whatever *that* means. Oh, he threw in all his usual disclaimers—about how none of it was a hard and fast map of my life. Advised me that if I was prudent, I could avoid catastrophes—things like being accused of Alanna's murder, maybe."

Russ lunged to his feet and paced back and forth, visibly working off tension. By the time he spoke again, he sounded almost calm. "While it was happening, everything seemed unreal. The cops were very polite. Never came right out and accused me, understand? For one thing, thanks to my service record and being a gun owner, my fingerprints are already on file, and my past had been thoroughly checked years ago. If I hadn't been clean, I wouldn't have a permit for some of the firearms in this house. But . . . all the same, they asked a *hell* of a lot of questions."

Feeling as though she were stepping into deep, dangerous water, Holly said gently, "Russ, may *I* ask a question? You don't have to answer. Maud said you found Alanna's body. How did that happen?"

157

His face was a bleak mask. "She was going to file for divorce. Told me nothing would change her mind, this time."

So, Kyle's dream of pulling up stakes had failed. Thinking out loud, Holly murmured, "He didn't mention divorce, just plans to go to California—"

"That was earlier," Russ said impatiently. "The whole idea fell flat. Never would have worked out, anyway, with Sylvia in the picture; she'd have followed them anywhere on earth. It was made all the more complicated by the financial mess at Preis Enterprises, just before Kyle's dad . . . well, what happened was accepted as an accident. But a lot of people around here believe he committed suicide. Maybe it was Dan's way of solving his money troubles. I guess we'll never know, for sure. The insurance investigators couldn't prove anything was amiss, and the settlement bailed out the publishing company, at least for the time being."

Holly nodded, recalling similar comments she'd heard elsewhere.

The artist drew a deep breath and returned to her main question. "I'd been at the Martins' all that evening, fine-tuning details for a show at their gallery. On impulse, I decided to stop by Kyle's place and have things out, once and for all. It wasn't until . . . until later that I found out Kyle wasn't even home that night. He was still in Chicago when the police finally were able to notify him . . .."

Russ's fiery gaze fixed on a point past Holly's right shoulder. "Alanna was dead when I got to the house. Had been dead at least an hour, according to the medical examiner. That's one of the things that saved my ass from a murder charge; the Martins could testify I'd been at their place till fifteen minutes before I called 911 from Kyle's. Lord help me, if I'd been with her—"

"You might be dead, too."

"Maybe." His focus—and Holly's—shifted to the gun on the coffee table.

"Were . . . were you armed . . . I mean . . . that night?"

"I often am."

It was, at the very least, an evasive answer. Holly was uncertain what to say. He saved her the trouble of deciding. "There's something I wanted to ask *you*—"

The telephone's ring cut off the rest of the sentence. Russ growled an expletive and went to the wall phone beside the door. His side of the conversation shifted from a snapped, "Hello," to a tooth-gritting, insincere apology. In the exchange that followed he confined himself to "yes," "no," and "sorry about that." When he hung up his expression was one of sour irritation. "Damn! Baskins never *can* keep his schedule straight. Now he claims the deadline on that cover is *tomorrow* instead of Wednesday. I'll have to work like hell to finish the thing. Sorry. And after I invited you . . ." His anger softened into regret. He eyed Holly like a child denied a promised treat.

"It's all right. Really. I understand. You have to make a living. Believe me, I appreciate that motive. Besides, we *did* finish the shooting lesson. And I've been intending to take a walk around the lake. Toby tells me it's not much of a hike, and the weather's beautiful today. I ought to get more exercise, anyway. Just sitting around Stephen's office all day . . . I'm out of shape."

"Not from where I'm standing."

When she'd first met Russ Graham, Holly thought his burning stare was lustful ogling. Later, she'd decided that she'd misread him. Now, her first impression was rekindled. There was no mistaking the look he gave her.

"No need for improvement, not in my books. Hey, let me at least fix you some lunch first. Wait till I put the gun away."

He quickly climbed to the bedroom loft and placed the holstered weapon on a bedside table.

As he descended, Holly remarked, "That's fine for discouraging unwelcome visitors at night, but what if they come in the daytime?"

As Russ laid out sandwich makings in the kitchenette, he replied with cold-blooded practicality, "I'd yank one of my long guns off the wall and cave in their heads."

Holly winced at the answer, and at his clumsy efforts to play chef. She took the chore away from him and deftly assembled a light snack. Over lunch, they swapped views of their mutual employer, Stephen, made plans to attend a Lake Michigan regatta the following weekend, and a shooting exhibition two weekends after that.

When they were done, Russ insisted on walking Holly out to the hiking trail before he began painting. He led the way up the gravel drive to the point where the path crossed it. Russ halted there and pointed. "This follows the lakeshore all the way around. In a few places, the blacktop road practically joins it, but most of the time that'll be uphill and off to your right. Just stick with the trail, and it'll shave close to half a mile off the distance."

"Thanks. I'll remember that. Well, I'd better be going, so you can get to work."

His hand brushed hers tentatively, but he hastily withdrew from the contact. Not a toucher. Or . . . perhaps his behavior was evidence of dogged loyalty to Alanna Preis's memory. How did one cope with a rival who was a dead woman?

Rival? Now why had she thought of *that* word?

On impulse, Holly stood on tiptoe and pecked his cheek. Russ stiffened a moment, and then a slow smile lit up his face. She winked and said, "Thanks for the shooting lessons," and started walking eastward.

"My pleasure!" he shouted after her. "Let's do it again, soon. And I'll make damned sure Baskins won't pull this stunt and spoil things, the *next* time!"

Holly looked back, waving good-bye. Russ continued to stand where she'd left him, staring after her until a bend in the path blocked their view of one another.

As promised, the weather was fine. Brilliant afternoon sunlight reflected off dancing waves to her left. Further out in the lake, rowboats bobbed at anchor, and fishermen, still as statues, watched their lines, hoping for a bite. In a roped-off area at the far western end of the lake, swimmers splashed and dived.

Here, at the southeastern curve of the lakeshore, the foot path was carpeted with polished gravel and designed for easy walking. The trail rarely strayed far from the water, and then only to make a short detour around a lakefront property. Occasionally the path briefly merged with Dark Lake's two-lane blacktop road, but each time it did so, it soon veered downhill again and resumed its course along the beach.

Holly noted familiar names on mailboxes lining the road. She was gradually acquiring an overall picture, a sort of mental aerial photograph, of the community. That sprawling mansion across the way was Maud's. And there, two nearly identical rambling brick ranches, their lawns divided by a hedge—those were Kyle's and Sylvia's homes. With a blink of surprise, Holly turned and peered southwest, spotting the Detloff complex on its tree shrouded hill. Stephen really *did* live but a short distance from his publishers. The road meandered so much it was difficult to realize how close to each other individual properties lay. Holly recalled the night of the Martins' party, when Bianca had shuddered as they passed Kyle's house; at the time, that trip seemed to take much longer than it must have in actuality.

Of course, Kyle wasn't home today. He'd be at that golfing tournament, somewhere north of Chicago. As Holly passed the Preis mansions she noted that both houses appeared deserted. *That* was a relief; she'd worried that Sylvia might be home. It would be that woman's style to fling open the door, call out to her, and demand that she come in to chat. Happily, nothing of the sort occurred. Holly wondered if Sylvia knew how hard people tried to avoid her. Probably not. Such personalities were generally dead to other persons' feelings.

Not only the Preis houses were deserted this afternoon. A lot of residents seemed to be away, perhaps on Sunday excursions to the area's numerous summer festivals; any given weekend in the Region, as it was called locally, offered a variety of fairs, musical extravaganzas, flea markets, auctions, or other entertainments. Even a small combination grocery and grill at the extreme east end of the lake was closed, with a "Gone Fishing" sign posted on its door. All of the trail's lovely scenery might have been reserved for Holly's sightseeing pleasure alone.

As she began to head west, the blacktop veered away sharply from the lake, going up a slope and out of sight. From that point on, only a narrow gravel lane provided access to the cottages and houses near the lake. Holly continued hiking down the paralleling foot trail, picking a few wildflowers. They wouldn't last long, of course, but how beautiful they were!

A grove of willows grew right down to the lake's edge, and she had to duck under the hanging branches to continue. When she emerged from their green shadows, she was surprised to see that beyond the grove the foot path split into three indistinct meanders. Which was the correct one? After a moment, Holly decided to stay with the trail closest to the water.

She felt proud. Although she surely must have walked more than a mile by now, she wasn't a bit tired. But she *was* getting hot. What had happened to that pleasant breeze she'd enjoyed earlier? The afternoon suddenly had turned oppressive. Not a breath of air stirred.

Scorpio House on its forested hill was clearly visible, dominating the southern shore directly opposite her position. It looked like a castle looming above a medieval village. As its lord and master dominated Dark Lake's society? Stephen Detloff and those who were bound to him—by love, economics, or loyalty—certainly loomed very large in *her* new life.

The blup-blup sound of fish skimming the water's surface brought Holly back to things in her immediate vicinity. Birds trilled and insects chirped. She might as well be in an isolated state park. All signs of human habitation had vanished. With a start, she saw that the path was about to disappear, too. Nobody—not Toby, and not Russ—had warned her that the trail split at the willow grove. Plainly, she'd chosen the wrong fork. And now, directly ahead of her, there was only the barest excuse for a track, snaking among high dunes.

At this point, she ought to be more than halfway around the lake. What was that ominous phrase they used in disaster movies? *Past the point of no return.*

In theory, if she went on past the dunes, she *should* find the main path again, on the far side. And that *should* lead her back to the blacktop road and to Scorpio House.

At any rate, there was no sense in turning back. She started forward, slogging through increasingly loose sand. In a dismayingly short time, the path was gone.

Holly trudged into a labyrinth bordering the shore.

She wiped her forehead and peeled her sweaty tank-top away from her skin, fanning herself. There was absolutely no breeze. The air wasn't merely stagnant; it had become a palpable weight. And what had happened to the sunlight? The sky was a lowering, threatening grey blanket, as though a concrete ceiling was descending upon her.

Her steps dragging, she went on, trying to keep to what *seemed* to be the right course—until she reached a blowout. Much larger than the one surrounding Russ's studio home, this was a huge sprawl of sand, one side open to the lake. In a way, there was a stark beauty to the site, as if it were a natural sculpture. A relentless wind, working year after year, had created this . . .

The wind! It was rising so fast!

Holly pushed hair out of her eyes and stared up at the descending clouds. They chased each other, tumbling, swirling into ominous, peculiar scrolling shapes, writhing and twisting like snakes—a tortured Van Gogh painting, coming to life.

Immense thunderheads boiled up to the southwest. Even with her view partially blocked by the dunes, Holly could see jagged streaks of lightning ripping down from the clouds' bellies.

How could this have happened with so little warning?

What a stupid question! She was native to the Great Lakes region. She knew what a collision of Canadian air and Gulf moisture could do. Until now she'd been lucky, never having had to deal with tornados and their dreaded cousins—"damaging surface winds."

Obviously, her luck had run out.

The atmosphere was thick, stifling, and her ears felt strange. Air pressure was dropping rapidly!

Trying to think calmly, Holly considered her options.

No place to hide. Not *here*.

Swimmers and fishermen were racing for shore and shelter. Very sensible! She intended to stay well away from the lake, too! On the horizon, lightning cracked and thunder boomed, heading steadily toward the little community. Water and lightning were a deadly combination to anybody foolish enough to challenge them!

Holly looked back over her shoulder. If she tried to retrace her steps to a more populated area she'd lose a lot of time— and time seemed in dangerously short supply. She might be able to seek shelter in someone's house back to the east, *if* she could find anyone home. *If* she could get that far before the storm broke . . .

No. Better to keep going west and pick up the pace. She'd push herself hard and get to Scorpio House. Fifteen minutes, surely no more than twenty. She could do it!

But she hadn't considered the barrier she had to cross— those dunes.

Holly began to lose the battle the moment she started forward. Grit filled her shoes, blew into her clothing and mouth, tangled in her hair, and lashed at her face. She threw up an arm, shielding her eyes, plunging onward desperately.

The wind howled, rising to an eerie wail, as it built miniature sand tornadoes. Racing clouds blackened, forming an approaching squall line. Thunder now cracked almost simultaneously with each streak of lightning.

Grimly determined to make it to the road, Holly pushed on.

By now, her pulse was racing, nerves drawing taut, her senses preternaturally heightened. Every aspect of her surroundings and each tiny sensation seemed sharply magnified.

Suddenly, she froze in her tracks, listening intently. Hair rose on the back of her neck. She slewed around, peering through sand-speckled air.

Had she only imagined she heard another sound besides the wind and thunder?

Shaken, Holly trudged on through blown and drifted sand

for another twenty or thirty feet. Then she halted once more, adrenaline flowing.

She wasn't mistaken. That sound definitely was *not* the wind. Apprehension turned to anger. "Who is it?" she shouted. "I can hear your footsteps. Come on! Show yourself!"

The dunes were perfect hiding places, if someone didn't want to be seen.

"Who *is* it?" Holly repeated, louder.

No answer.

Feeling cold despite the sticky air, she hurried on. Not much further, surely!

Just a short distance beyond these dunes. If she could only reach the blacktop road . . .

Footsteps! A gritty, muffled, clumping sound.

Holly spun and yelled into a sandy fog. "Who is it? Why don't you answer me?" The only response was the howling wind.

Growing panic nibbled at her spine with sharp little teeth. Someone was following her, someone who refused to show himself—or herself. Unwillingly, she thought of Alanna Preis, and of Ivor Wilcox's all-too-frequent, grisly recitations of facts about the serial murders. Had the Butcher Knife Murderer ever struck in daylight? Was he—or she—on the verge of trying a first-time experiment?

The effort of pushing her feet through sand slowed Holly's pace to a near-crawl. She managed to reach a tall dune outcrop studded with crumbling rock. Panting, she collapsed against it, scraping her palms as she fell onto its unyielding surface. Ignoring the resulting flash of hot pain, she again looked back over her shoulder.

Was there a hulking shadow darting to cover behind another dune? She couldn't be certain.

But now she saw something else she hadn't noticed before—a beached rowboat a hundred yards or so east. She was sure it hadn't been there earlier when she'd passed by that spot.

Did it belong to her unknown pursuer?

Dark Lake was large enough to grant any boater anonymity. No one would pay attention if someone put a craft in the water on a balmy Sunday afternoon.

An almost deafening clap of thunder made Holly flinch. The wind blasted her with yet more sand. The sky was black, and a few sharp spatters of rain stung her flesh.

She had to get to Scorpio House.

Now!

Fighting the sand and wind, she ran. The elements pounded at her mercilessly. Holly leaned into the gale, struggling, breath heaving in and out of her lungs.

Did she hear frenzied panting behind her?

Mustn't look back!

Run!

Flying grit all but blinded her, but she refused to stop. Her mind locked onto a mantra: *Keep going. Keep running!*

She did . . .

Until the sandy ground abruptly vanished, leaving emptiness beneath her feet.

Chapter 10

Holly half fell, half slid down a slope into an eight-foot deep hole. As she struck bottom, her left foot twisted at right angles just as she bore her weight upon it. Pain lanced through the joint as she crumpled into a sprawl.

Somehow, despite shock, she clung to one overriding thought: *She must not cry out.* In this near-tornadic fury, her pursuer might overlook her—*if* she kept silent.

Tears flowed, and Holly bit her lip. Clutching her foot, she gently rocked back and forth, trying to soothe the hurt as she had when she was younger—a brave little tomboy.

She *must* be quiet. Her very life might well depend upon that.

Above her, the wind continued to roar.

Then . . . footsteps. Very close to the pit where she sat. A scuffling noise. Feet plodding through dense sand.

Holly held her breath. A gigantic fist seemed to close around her heart.

The footsteps went toward the lakeside, moving past her hiding place.

Whenever the storm permitted, she could hear heavy breathing, then an occasional pause, as though the unseen stranger was taking stock. Searching? Conjecturing where she'd disappeared to?

Dear God, help me! Please!

Eternity lasted at least five minutes, while that menacing presence lurked nearby. Then the footsteps changed direction, moving . . . away! The sounds grew fainter and fainter, finally lost amid the wind's roar.

She hadn't been seen! And she would have been such easy prey, trapped here.

Something scuttled across her hand. Holly gasped and jerked back reflexively—moving her injured ankle. Fresh pain stabbed at her. Through tear-blurred vision, she saw a tiny sand crab fleeing, burrowing into the sand pit's side to escape the terrible human. Torn between hysterical laughter and fear of making any noise—lest her pursuer come back!—Holly sagged, and darkness closed over her, taking consciousness with it.

When she came to, she was gazing up into the last moments of the storm. A few final rain drops fell on her wet face, mingling with her tears. She lay on her back. Overhead, clouds were breaking up, patches of blue starting to appear.

Slowly, biting her lip, Holly sat up. She was drenched. Mild hysteria made her giggle inanely. Talk about not knowing enough to get in out of the rain! Then relief swept over her. She was alive! The pursuer, like the storm, was gone!

Gradually, pulling together her frayed nerves, she assessed her situation. She had to get back to Scorpio House. Somehow. Stephen and Bianca would be wondering what had happened to her. They'd call Russ and learn when she'd left his studio.

When *had* she left there? Holly had no idea how long she'd lain unconscious or how long the storm had lasted.

First things first. Listen. She heard nothing but birdsong and insect chatter. Nature returning to an ordinary summer afternoon, its air washed clean by wind and rain. No sound of footsteps. No heavy breathing.

So . . . time to get out of the pit. An interesting trick, that, with a useless ankle!

Holly studied her prison. One wall of the hole was less steep than the rest of it. Carefully, favoring her injury, she crawled over to that gentle slope. The sand there was still wet with rain, giving it just enough cohesion for her to gain purchase. Inching her way up, resting often on dirt and rock outcroppings, she finally managed to reach the top.

For several minutes, she lay on the pit's edge, waiting for her throbbing ankle to quiet down. Then, warily, she peered around. She was utterly alone.

And not over twenty feet from the lake.

Now that the storm had abated, she could also see the blacktop road. No more than a hundred feet away! If only she could have spotted that sooner!

It would have been so easy, running on a hard, smooth surface . . . but it would have been easy running for her pursuer, as well! Fate, tumbling her into that pit, had provided her only true chance of escape!

Slowly regaining energy, Holly staggered upright, leaning against a dune hummock of sand and grass. Gingerly, she lowered her left foot—and promptly fell on her face. For a while she breathed through her teeth and moaned, regretting her rashness.

Getting onto her hands and knees, she began to crawl toward the road. Holly bent her left knee at an awkward angle to make sure her foot didn't touch the ground and trigger another explosion of pain.

What a ludicrous picture she must make! Creeping along like a baby!

She had almost reached the pavement when she heard a squeal of brakes and car doors slamming. Holly lifted her head. An enormous, boxy vehicle had come to a stop a short distance from her. People piled out, running toward her.

"Pet! What's the matter? What happened?" Bianca, Ivor

Wilcox, and Toby swarmed around Holly. More sedately, Maud and Cynthia Martin brought up the rear.

Holly tried to laugh, wiping at her tear-streaked face. "It's the silliest thing . . ." she began, suddenly deciding to lie. She couldn't speak of that terrifying pursuit. Not just yet. "I . . . I was taking a walk around the lake when I got caught in the storm. I fell in a sand pit. Back there," she said and waved vaguely. "Twisted my ankle."

While Cynthia examined the injured joint, Maud shook her head and said, "You were sure lucky!"

"Sure was!" Ivor agreed. "Just heard on the radio— weather bureau confirmed it was a tornado—touched down ten miles south. We got the edge of it. But even so, you could have been killed by flying debris—"

"Oh, don't say such things!" Bianca said with a shudder. Touched, Holly brushed her sister's cheek as Bianca went on, "It's a miracle she's okay. A miracle!"

Indeed. Perhaps it was, though not for the reasons Bianca imagined. Holly acknowledged inwardly that the storm had been her salvation, its concealing wind and rain, and the pit, providing a haven from an unknown pursuer.

"What are we going to do?" Bianca cried, wringing her hands.

"Well, she doesn't want to sit on the roadside all day, silly," Maud said briskly. "Come on. What are you ninnies thinking of? We need to get her to a doctor. For Pete's sake, you clowns, do I have to do everything? You two men make a chair out of your arms and carry her to the car. Weren't either of you ever in the Boy Scouts?"

"No way!" Ivor retorted with a tigerish grin. "My crowd ran to a different sort of recreational activities." He smirked knowingly at Toby. But the pair followed Maud's instructions and got Holly into the car with only minimal difficulty.

On the way to the emergency room, Bianca called Stephen on her cell phone, and the astrologer met the rest at the hospital. By then Holly was thoroughly embarrassed by all the fuss and bother, particularly after she had seen people hurt in the tornado being treated. After a lot of paperwork and tedious waiting, X-rays revealed she had suffered a sprain, not a broken ankle. A slender, dark bearded resident eventually let her escape with a generous supply of painkillers and advice to apply rest, ice, compresses, and moderate exercise.

Holly made the trip back to Scorpio House in Maud's "green elephant," a wise choice, since that vehicle was far more comfortable than Stephen's. Dark Lake's mother hen drove carefully over bumps and around curves, coddling her passenger. Warmed by the older woman's kindness, Holly at last allowed herself to relax.

Hours later, though, Bianca continued to hover over her anxiously. "Are you feeling any better?"

Holly lay propped up in bed, ankle wrapped in ice packs and scraped palms treated and bandaged. "I'm fine. Cozy." And that was so, in a way. Holly was safe in her own room. The ordeal in the storm almost seemed like a bad dream. But it hadn't been. Even painkillers couldn't erase her memories of terror. On the way to the hospital she'd seen graphic evidence of the tornado's fury—mobile homes destroyed, roofing and house siding strewing lawns, trees uprooted. Perhaps she'd been in as much danger from the storm as from her pursuer . . .

Somehow she doubted that.

"I'm much better now, thank you, Bianca. Everyone's been wonderful."

"It's too bad all this had to spoil your nice walk."

"And your day. Didn't you say you and Cynthia were going to write up an account of your tea for the local newspaper?" Holly hinted. Her sister's sincere concern was touching, but, typically, Bianca was overdoing it.

"Are you really sure it'll be all right?" The door eased open and Stephen slipped into the room, regarding the scene with a reserved expression as Bianca persisted, "Isn't there something I can get for you, do for you?"

As Holly smiled feebly and brushed aside the offer, Stephen said, "Don't worry, My Own. I imagine what she most needs now is rest. Do go on downstairs, love. Cynthia is waiting for you. I'll stay with Holly."

Bianca brightened, though she eyed the invalid uncertainly. "Well, if you're sure." She patted Holly's hand and rose, pausing to kiss Stephen on her way out. When she had gone, he drew up a chair beside the bed and sat down.

"What a change," Holly murmured, "one very much for the better. She's definitely not as selfish as she used to be. More focused, more . . . mature. You're quite the Pygmalion."

Stephen's deep-set, mesmerizing gaze pinned her like a butterfly. "What really happened out there? Won't you confide in me?"

She shivered, feeling a chill that owed nothing to Scorpio House's superb air conditioning system. "What do you mean?"

"Call it intuitive insight, or the planets I was born under. Something far worse than a twisted ankle has happened to you, worse even than being caught in that awful storm."

He seemed to be all-knowing, the ultimate sorcerer, a man who just possibly might be able to see into the future. Could he see into hers? She wanted to believe that, to find reassurance. For good or ill, she needed to trust *someone*. During these past weeks, she'd had ample opportunities to watch Stephen at his work, and in his daily interactions with others.

His manner was consistently benign, caring, and rich with sympathy. The sea-change he'd caused in Bianca's behavior was but one testimony to his power to affect and help other people.

On impulse, with childlike faith, Holly emptied her fears into the magician's hands. Words poured from her, mingling with a fresh flood of tears repressed until that very moment. She gave him all of it: Nightmares, the near drowning at the picnic, her recurrent premonitions, and ended by describing the terrifying cat-and-mouse game among the dunes. Then, completely spent, she lay back on the pillows, feeling as if she had divested herself of the weight of the world.

Stephen's dark eyes were wide with shock. All the worries that had afflicted her were now his to share. "You saw the boat clearly? Could you read a name, a license number?" he asked. Plainly, he hoped to track the craft to its owner. His face fell when Holly shook her head. "And the incident at the picnic. You're sure it wasn't just . . . just a prank that got out of hand?"

"It was far more than a prank." She noted Stephen's reaction and went on, "You're thinking of Sylvia, aren't you? Lord knows I have no love for the woman, but I really don't believe it was her. Whoever tried to drown me was extremely strong. I doubt she has that kind of muscles. And surely she wouldn't have . . . wouldn't have kissed me," Holly finished with some embarrassment.

"She has a *terrible* Saturn," the astrologer said morosely. "It clashes with Kyle's chart, just as it did with her late husband's. Inevitable, I suppose, since they all have—in Dan's case, *had*—seriously afflicted conjunctions. In a way, Sylvia suffers from an almost unquenchable drive to dominate every life she touches. She nearly succeeded with Alanna—"

"Before Alanna tried to break free . . . and was killed."

Holly was appalled by the direction of her thoughts. "Stephen, is my chart like Alanna's? I had all those dreams involving . . . involving the sign of Scorpio. Did you forecast danger for Alanna, too?"

His sorcerer's face was bleak. "My dear, I deal in possibilities, not unavoidable fate. I have never yearned more than I do at this moment for the omnipotence that some people credit me with. Despite publicity, I'm hardly an all-knowing demi-god. I'm only a man with a certain talent for astrology. I trade in potentials, not hard and fast predictions. Only fools make those. I wish I could answer your questions, but I can't." In a sad tone he added, "I wish, too, that I could wave a wand and make all your troubles disappear, but I can't do that, either."

"Can you at least tell me whether those troubles will get worse?"

"I don't know. As I recall your chart, at present you're going through a critical period. Your father's death, of course, and moving here, taking on a new job, meeting new people. There's a shift of influence out of your fourth house—an end to your loving filial servitude and obligations. You stored up great karmic treasure, my dear, by your devotion to your father. But now it looks as though you may have to cope with a very different sort of ordeal, one entangled with your Venus and Moon." He forced a smile and added, "In other words, danger mixed with romance."

Holly refused to accept his attempt to lighten the situation. "And death? Stephen, why am I so obsessed with the Butcher Knife Murderer? I'm worse than Ivor Wilcox. He, at least, has an understandable interest in the case. But me? I can't seem to push it out of my mind, awake or sleeping."

She longed for her wizardly brother-in-law to laugh and tell her she was merely imagining things. Instead, Stephen wouldn't meet her gaze. He toyed absently with the beside phone cord and murmured, "Like me, you are a sensitive. I think that has aroused your survival instincts—as a defense against the danger in your forecast. That's good. Use it! It's a tool that can help you through whatever is to come. You must admit that it's aided you in dodging disaster so far. Agreed?" He finally looked directly at her, and this time his smile wasn't forced. "Remember, I'm not making predictions, only reading warnings in your chart."

"Stephen, someone's tried to kill me at least once—at the picnic. Now this latest scare was quite probably another attempt on my life. That's way beyond 'warnings.' What should I do? Hide in bed for the rest of my life?"

"That's not your nature, is it?" he asked, his smile broadening.

He was right. And despite her profound skepticism about his profession, she had to concede that he'd been honest with her. Well, star-crossed "crisis period" or not, she resolved that all of this was *not* going to keep her down.

"Rest. Think it over," Stephen advised. "Whatever you decide, I'll do my best to help. You have only to ask." He sighed heavily. "It's ironic that my wealth is of absolutely no use in dealing with your problem."

Moved, Holly said, "These past few weeks have been a dream come true for me. A fairy tale existence. And fairy tales always have a few ogres and demons lurking about, don't they? But in the end, things generally come out okay. Don't they? I'm sure all of this will eventually change for the better."

"Good girl! Good little Virgo Moon. Wholehearted stick-to-itiveness! That's the ticket!" As he got to his feet she wondered if those words were sincere or whether he was just trying to boost her spirits. Then Stephen went on, "If you aren't too tired, do you feel up to seeing a visitor? A very con-cerned young man has been cooling his heels out in the hall for some time. Shall I send him in?"

Holly nodded. But it wasn't until he ushered Russ into the room that she realized how very much she had longed to see those pale eyes and that sharp face.

Stephen laughed, saying a bad ankle would serve as a chaperone, and left them alone.

For a long moment, she and Russ stared silently at one an-other. "I should have gone with you," he said at last, remorse putting strain on his voice. "These damned summer storms! I should have . . . Ivor told me what happened . . ."

Holly extended a hand to him, and he took it gently in both of his, careful with her bandaged palm. "I'm all right now. I just have to stay off my foot for a while."

"You're sure? Dammit, I'm responsible. I'd never forgive myself if—"

"Did you get your painting done?"

"What? Oh . . . yeah. I—"

"Anybody home?" It was Kyle. He had taken a step into the room, then stopped cold, staring at Russ. The publisher's handsome features clouded with surprise. A flush crept up his face to his tousled hair. "I . . . uh . . . didn't know you had company."

Trying to sound bright and chipper, Holly said, "Come on in. How was your tournament?"

Kyle approached her bed, nervously shifting a florist's box from one hand to the other. "What? Oh, it got rained out. Same storm that hit here. So I drove back. Just heard about . . . are you okay, Princess?"

"A little ruffled around the edges," she said, thoroughly tired of talking about her recent close call.

Kyle's focus locked on the pair's joined hands. Then,

putting on a cheery face, he laid the florist's box on the vanity. "Just a few American beauties. Sweets to the sweet, and all that . . ."

"Thank you so much," Holly said. The words came out slurred. Unable to smother a yawn, she muttered, "I . . . I guess wha'ever th' doctor gave me is startin' to hit . . ."

The men, suddenly ill at ease, edged away from her. Russ looked simultaneously sympathetic and uncomfortable. The publisher seemed distressed. Holly often had seen her father's cronies reacting the same way to one of his "bad spells." Many men didn't seem to handle illness and injury well at all, whether as patients or caregivers.

Kyle jittered, backing toward the door. "Oh? Yeah . . . sure! Just dropped by to see how you were, Princess. Look, I'll stop by again tomorrow. Okay? Russ, good to see you," he said, offering his hand. With obvious reluctance, Russ accepted. Kyle turned to Holly once more and said loudly, "Now, you take care of yourself." And with that, he turned and fled.

The artist stared after him a second, then said, "I'd better be going, too. Let you get some sleep."

"Not yet, please," Holly said, fighting drowsiness. "You . . . you don't like him, do you? You haven't forgiven him."

"It isn't that." Russ looked surprised by his own statement. "That's true. I guess time, and a lot of other things, burned it out of me. It's like something that happened a long time ago, to three other people. Right now, I'm not sure exactly how I feel about Kyle. He's been real buddy-buddy with me lately. Came over to the studio a couple of times to give me commissions for book covers. Good fat fees, too. I'm not sure Preis Enterprises can afford that right now, frankly. Nevertheless, I ought to be grateful. But . . . well, he reminds me of a live grenade."

"Yes. Yes, that's it. I occasionally feel the same way about him."

Russ grinned wryly. "I could put up with him a lot easier if he wasn't so hell bent on shaking hands constantly."

"He's a toucher. You're not." Holly heaved a sigh, her eyelids drooping. "But I like that. I'm slow to make up m'mind, too, sometimes . . ."

"Stephen probably would explain it all with astrology."

"Something romantic about our Suns and Moons . . ." she whispered dreamily.

Russ briefly touched her hand once more and said, "I'll beat it now . . ."

When he released her, Holly felt as though a lifeline had been jerked out of her grasp. Rousing, she exclaimed, "Wait, please!" She dredged her brain for what she'd intended to say. Finally, the errant thought drifted past her frontal lobes and she snatched at it. "Would you do something for me?"

"Sure. What?" No hesitation. For all Russ knew, she was going to ask him to row out into the lake and drown himself.

"I want to read Ivor's notes, if he doesn't mind. That book on the murderer. Tell him I'll take good care of the files."

The artist's face darkened. "Why on earth . . . no, never mind. I'll ask him. He and Toby have been so busy elsewhere lately that I think Ivor's goofing off with his writing, anyway. I'll make copies, so you won't need to worry about losing any pages. But . . ." and he stared at her with concern, "I sure as hell can think of better get-well cards."

"Please. I really want to read them." Her words mushed together badly. By now, her limbs seemed separate from her body and her eyelids weighted with bricks.

"Just rest." Russ's voice sounded faint in her ears. A roughened hand touched her face. Rough—the skin hardened from the harsh chemicals of an artist's profession. A kiss

179

brushed her lips. The contact was so delicate she couldn't be certain it wasn't a drug-induced illusion. Both caress and kiss had been gentle as an angel's benediction.

Not a toucher. But sometimes . . .

For the first time in weeks, Holly's nightmares were gone, replaced by REM sleep idylls in lush green fields beside a lake's silvery waters.

The following days were a strange mix of boredom, frustration at the slow pace of recuperation, and pleasure. Forced to pamper her injury, she grew increasingly restless at being confined to the mansion. In compensation, Russ Graham and Kyle Preis dropped by frequently to visit her. There were other well-wishers, too—Maud, the Martins, Toby, Ivor Wilcox, and several new friends Holly had met during the past few weeks. But as she neared the end of her recovery, she was quite ready to resume a normal life. That would happen tomorrow, she announced, and Stephen and Bianca agreed.

Saturday, though, had been spent seeking fresh diversions. By late afternoon, that led her to the living room, where she migrated toward the piano. To Holly's surprise, Bianca joined her there, and the two of them enjoyed a relaxing hour reminiscing with music.

When Holly finished playing the last bar, her sister beamed and said, "I had almost forgotten that tune. Funny, the memories it brings."

"Yes, it does." Meeting her sister's warm smile, Holly nodded. Happy memories. Family. Childhood. The four of them in the living room of the little house in Norris Falls. Mother and Holly playing duets on the piano, Father and Bianca singing.

"I don't remember Mother very well," Bianca said wistfully. "But Father . . ."

Bittersweet love shone in her eyes. Every day was presenting new proof of Stephen Detloff's profound influence on
his bride. Holly was amazed and gratified to watch her sister's
steady progress toward more mature attitudes and a far less
self-absorbed personality. Bit by bit, the two women were
learning how to be real friends, for the first time in their lives.

"They were both good people. And those were good
times . . ."

"Come, come!" Stephen strode into the room. The late
afternoon sun streaming through the windows cast an aura
about his form, a spotlight greeting Scorpio's grand entrance.
He looked splendid in a beautifully tailored tuxedo and carried Bianca's expensive stole over one arm. "No gloomy
thoughts," he chided. "Not on such a peaceful evening. Are
you ready, My Own?"

"In a moment. I told Melanie I'd meet her date before
they left." A quick kiss for Stephen, a smiling glance at her
sister, and Bianca hurried off to fulfill the obligation to her
maid.

The astrologer ran his spidery fingers over the piano's
arm. "I heard you playing as I came down the hall. You have
such a gentle touch on the keys, very much like my sainted
mother's. Ah! This *is* a day for nostalgia, it seems!"

"And for accepting the past and looking into the future?"
Holly got to her feet and put the music back in the storage
rack. Her ankle still hurt a bit, but nothing like it had. Good
care and good sense had brought her back quickly to near
normalcy. "I've been meaning to tell you—you're the best
thing that could have happened to Bianca. Thank you for all
you've done for her, and for me."

He steepled his forefingers and regarded her thoughtfully.
"Are you sure you won't come with us?"

"Oh, no. This is your special night," Holly said, grinning.

Her sister had been chattering about little else recently. A banquet in Stephen's honor! Celebrities galore gathering at an exclusive Chicago club. Holly had no intention of intruding on such a triumphant and romantic outing.

Had she once actually been suspicious of her brother-in-law? In retrospect, that seemed foolish. The man was the soul of consideration, and a completely trustworthy confidant; he hadn't mentioned her confession to anyone. At one point, though, he *had* suggested consulting the police. Holly vetoed the idea quickly, imagining the sort of embarrassment that would involve!

"And just what proof do you have, lady, that someone tried to kill you? How about these women, Charlie? Nervous nellies, all of 'em. Seeing the Butcher Knife Murderer everywhere they look!"

"You won't be worried, here alone?" Stephen asked.

"Of course not. I feel quite safe in Scorpio House, thanks to all of Toby's locks and alarm systems."

"No date tonight, Sis?" Bianca called from the foyer. Stephen turned and hurried to her side, his eyes alight. Holly followed him to the entryway. As he draped the fur over Bianca's shoulders, she winked at the younger woman and said, "I do hope your beaux haven't forgotten you, the fickle brutes!"

Amused, Holly replied, "Since we've been tripping over both of them lately, I hardly think I've been forgotten. In fact, Kyle invited me to go with him to his key club this evening, but I didn't feel up to that yet. I suppose he dug into his little black book for an alternate . . ."

Stephen snorted. "Naturally. With his Venus in Sagittarius, he won't be tied down for long by any one woman."

"And Russ?" Bianca asked slyly. "Surely he doesn't work every Saturday."

"My Own!" Stephen cried in mock outrage. "Of course he

does, if he has an assignment. Didn't you know? He's a Taurean, the ultimate follower of old-fashioned work ethic!"

Holly laughed, agreeing, grateful that Stephen's devotion to his profession was so often leavened by humor. "You're so right. When there's a deadline to be met, Russ always puts that first. I wouldn't have it any other way."

"I'm sure you wouldn't," he said, winking conspiratorially.

Before they departed, Bianca embraced her sister gently and said, "We'll try not to be too late."

"Stay as long as you like. Have a good time . . ."

Holly waited by the door until the sedan was out of sight. Then she carefully set the locks. Toby hadn't left the mansion yet, but the servants had the night off, and it seemed prudent to take precautions.

She went back into the living room and looked out toward the lake. The peaceful evening out there made her adventure in the dunes seem like a child's exaggerated fantasy. Was she really sure someone had been pursuing her with evil intent? Maybe it all had been a product of her imagination, stimulated by the approaching storm. That incident at the picnic was harder to brush aside, but that, too, now was less frightening. Perhaps it had, after all, been just a prank that got out of hand. Maybe, sometime in the future, the prankster would admit the indiscretion and apologize. If so, she'd be able to look back on all these events like a piece of fiction that had happened to someone else.

Later, though, up in her room, an irresistible urge drove her toward the bureau. There she opened a drawer and pulled out the bulging file folder Russ had brought her earlier in the week. Holly sat and began to read—again.

Ivor's research continued to cast a spell over her. Against her better judgment, she spent far too much time studying this horrifying material. His notes included portraits of the victims, Alanna Preis and the others. Why had they died? What terrible mistake brought each of them to a violent end? Had they been trapped? How? By someone they trusted? And then . . . the dreadful confrontation, the drawn knife, the realization that death stared them in the face . . .

Was the killer insane? Holly leafed through Ivor's scribbled, often cryptic notes. *He* didn't believe the murderer was mad. Well, not exactly. Wilcox pointed out that every case showed careful, calculated preparation. Until, at a crucial moment, by all the evidence, advance planning was abandoned. The killer went beserk, killing in a frenzy.

The women were stabbed repeatedly, even after their lives had fled.

According to a police profiler, the killer was male, and the nature of the murders bespoke a motive of perverted sexuality. Holly tended to agree, remembering abnormal psychology texts she'd read while seeking ways of handling her father's mental illness.

What drove the Butcher Knife Murderer? Why did he—or she—kill?

Ivor's analysis was blunt: *"This dude sure hates women. Maybe got crossed up good sometime past. By a sweetheart? Wife? Mother? Work that angle into the book.*

"He hates their guts—all women, not just the one behind his rage. Transference, the shrinks call it. Getting even with her by killing other women. Can't kill the one he really hates. Why? Is she dead? Too sacred to touch? The Madonna/whore theme? When he kills them, is he killing her, vicariously? Refer to Jack the Ripper here. Must set up an interview with Police Chief J . . ."

There was a knock on the door. Startled, Holly glanced up from the files and called out, "Come in." Belatedly, in light of what she'd just read, she wondered if she'd made a mistake— a bad one.

Toby entered, and she let out a sigh of relief. The computer expert looked at banks of flowers decorating the room and raised an eyebrow.

"I'm afraid Kyle tends to overdo it. How many gifts would he bring if I'd broken my leg, instead of merely sprained an ankle?" Holly asked, chuckling.

"All these from him? Yeah, when he falls—which he rarely does—he thinks the sky's the limit." Toby frowned, then shook off whatever had disturbed him. "Maud just called. She and Ivor will be here in a couple of minutes. Thought I'd see if there's anything you need before I leave."

"Going to another literary soiree? Ivor ought to get a Pulitzer if only for his ability to answer inane questions from his adoring fans."

"Yeah, he's lapping it up like a little kid. It means a lot to him, you know," Toby said with a grin. "Maud's been a real doll—introducing him all over the area and talking him up with her literary connections, and believe me, she's got plenty."

"I don't doubt it. Ivor's her latest mother hen project. I'm glad for him, and for you." Holly meant every word. Toby had really come alive since Ivor's arrival. That faint undercurrent of former tragedy still clung to the little man. But nowadays he tended to whistle while he worked.

"Thanks. You're one of the good ones, Holly." Then he frowned again, seeing what she held. "Are those copies of Ivor's notes? Why are you reading those? They'll give you nightmares."

Stephen said that Holly's astrological chart "bleshed" well with Toby's, making them good co-workers. She'd found that to be true. And despite skepticism she had to admit her brother-in-law might have something there. The affectionate concern in Toby's question was obvious.

Shrugging, Holly said, "I guess it's the appeal of the flame to the moth."

"I just don't think you ought to mess with that stuff. Too grim. Too bloody. Bad vibes all around. Reminds me of . . ." He broke off his train of thought. "Well, I'd better get downstairs before Maud leans on the horn. I'll set all the locks before I go. Only you, I, and Stephen have keys. You going to be okay now?"

"Fine. There's a TV movie I want to watch."

Toby nodded approvingly. "Lots better entertainment than those files. So long. Take it easy."

As he left, she peered down at the pages, thinking over what he'd said.

Nightmares. Of a looming figure with a knife, and the symbol of Scorpio hanging over her recurring vision. The preceding days, and a fast deepening interest in Russ Graham, had absorbed her attentions, almost banishing those bad dreams.

But not quite.

A vague disquiet haunted her every morning when she awoke. As if she had indeed suffered the recurring nightmare, but daylight chased it from conscious memory.

From the appearance of the files, Ivor Wilcox had collected everything it was possible to amass regarding the Butcher Knife Murderer. It was all here, but there was no definitive answer. No name to put to a killer who had made a widower of Kyle and a grieving lover of Russ, no one to blame for the other victims' deaths.

Scorpio, and nightmares. Why had Toby brought those fears back to vivid life? Or *was* it his fault? It could be the fault of these damned files. Annoyed with herself, Holly tossed aside the copy pages.

The bedside phone shrilled, startlingly loud. Surprised,

Holly peered at her watch. It was too early for Russ's nightly call. He wouldn't be finished working until nine, and it wasn't even eight yet.

On the second ring, she lifted the receiver. "Hello?" She heard a peculiar scratching noise and labored breathing. "H . . . hello?" she repeated, suddenly uneasy.

Very faintly, a tortured whisper: "Holly . . ."

Russ. Sounding strange, his voice distorted, as if he were struggling against some unknown force.

A stab of apprehension shot down her spine. "Russ? What's wrong?"

More labored breathing. "N . . . need help."

"Russ! What is it? Are you at the studio? Are you hurt?"

For a long moment, there was no response. Then she heard an achingly soft, "Yes."

"I'll get help! Call an ambulance!"

There was another pause, and then a whisper, almost inaudible amid that awful gasping, "Mustn't . . . Holly."

It was as though Russ could barely speak. Holly's heart constricted in frightened sympathy. He must be in terrible pain! "Russ, Russ! If you're hurt, you must have a doct—"

The line was dead. No, not dead. There was no dial tone. But she could no longer hear that sharp intake of breath. When she shouted frantically into the phone, there was no response.

As if the receiver had dropped from nerveless fingers, or were dangling uselessly, out of the reach of an injured, fallen man!

His guns! That image struck Holly like a bolt of lightning. She had read far too many reports of men cleaning supposedly "empty" guns, only to be seriously wounded or killed by those same weapons.

But Russ was so careful! Could he possibly have made a mistake? A fatal one?

187

No! She couldn't believe that! Wouldn't!

She ran to the window. From this vantage point on an upper floor she could see the roof of Russ's studio home. But that told her nothing. If he were hurt or dying, she wouldn't be able to see *him* from here!

And she couldn't call him back. Not with the line still open. Not if he were unable to speak!

Holly ran out into the hall and down the great stairs, shouting for aid. Panic overrode the lingering pain in her ankle. "Toby! Melanie! Clete!" Her cries echoed through empty rooms and halls.

Cold logic took control of her fear, forcing her to think clearly. Of course there was no reply! Everyone was gone for the evening. Her mind racing as she considered alternatives, Holly rushed into the offices and grabbed a phone. Those were different circuits than the one in her bedroom, so she could reach help this way . . .

Russ's whisper seemed to ring in her memory. *"Mustn't."*

Mustn't what? Call in outside help? Why? Stupid masculine pride? Or . . . was it a realistic fear that if she summoned EMTs, they would in turn notify the law? Russ was still very leery of the police, an understandable result of their investigation into Alanna's death. And . . . maybe he'd done something illegal tonight, something he didn't want discovered, even at the risk of his life. Weren't there all sorts of rules and regulations about his guns? Had he committed some kind of infraction? A mistake that got him hurt?

Whatever the reasons behind that "mustn't," she'd respect his plea to keep the law out of this, unless it was absolutely necessary. With effort, she cast aside her original impulse to phone for an ambulance.

But . . . now that she'd made that decision, what was she going to do next?

Help. Years of tending her father had given Holly a lot of practical nursing skills. She never dealt with a gunshot wound, but she *had* been forced to deal with a demented man whose strength often exceeded her own. She'd manage— somehow—to help Russ.

If he'd broken the law, no one else ever need know.

She cancelled the alarm on the solarium's outer door and hurried across the flagstone terrace. It was twilight, but she didn't yet need a flashlight to see her way.

An eerie, pearlescent Midwestern sunset glow hung over Dark Lake, giving everything she saw an air of unreality.

Limping, she tried to move quickly. No minor injury must betray her now. She'd coddle the abused joint later.

As she reached the blacktop road, Holly looked in both directions, hoping for aid. Nothing! Where was Maud, who tended to pop out of the woodwork at any other time?

Holly yearned for the big woman's no-nonsense presence. Maud would have helped her, and kept silent about any of Russ's transgressions. Then there'd be no need for him to worry about the police finding out.

Hobbling, she moved down the trail as fast as she could. Fear was a dragon, blowing hot flames against her back, thrusting her forward. She begged over and over, *"Please hold on until I can get there."*

She ran beneath trees casting long shadows. Out on the lake waves danced, their black waters crested with white-gold thrown by the sun's last rays—rays that now and then flashed at her blindingly. Stumbling ahead, she finally reached the blowout and pushed on across the sandy path, trying to run.

Then she was at the screen door, peering through its mesh, banging on its frame. "Russ! Russ! It's me! I'm here!" Before she could make a more serious attack on the obstacle, he came to the door.

He was unharmed, holding brushes and paintrags, and staring at her in bewilderment.

Whole and well! Not gasping for breath or pleading for help. Instead, he looked totally at a loss, plainly not understanding why she was standing there.

But it had been his voice on the phone! She would *swear* to that!

He opened the door to let her in. "What are you doing here? I *said* I'd call about nine . . ."

Suddenly, leather-clad fingers bit painfully into her arm, and shoved her inside the studio. Something cold and metallic pressed against her throat.

Holly sensed, with a kind of numb, sick certainty, that the object digging into her flesh was a knife.

Chapter 11

"Don't try anything stupid, Russ, or she gets it right now."

Her nightmare—coming true. Very slowly, she turned her head toward that shrill, almost hysterical voice.

Kyle. One gloved hand holding the knife, the other her arm.

Kyle, in the water beside her at the picnic, forcing her head under the waves.

Kyle, pursuing her through the storm.

Holly was beyond terror. She darted a glance at Russ. He stood frozen in the midst of an artist's tableau—easel, paints, and two bright floor lamps arranged to supplement the fading natural light. Graham looked first at Kyle, then at Holly, warily assessing the situation. His expression was taut with a desire to rescue her, and he moved very slightly.

"No! I said—don't try anything!" Kyle snarled. Holly noted that the publisher's handsome face glistened with sweat, as though he'd chased her all the way from Scorpio House. He had known she was coming here. Somehow, he had planned everything.

"Take it easy," Russ said, icily calm.

"Sure! I'll take it easy—*now!* That cute little recording fetched her right on the run, didn't it? You must have thought he was really dying, huh, Princess? It was quite a treat to see you trotting over here to check up on lover boy."

"Kyle . . ." Russ's eyes narrowed and his voice dropped into an achingly low register.

191

The other man continued to rant. "That little trick got you to open the door without a quibble, eh? And here we all are— nice and cozy. Private little tryst. Like all those trysts with Alanna, huh, Russ? Only this one's not so intimate."

Holly felt sick. She heard an all-too familiar note in Kyle's tirade, one she remembered from her father's demented ravings.

"I told you, time and again, I never touched Alanna," Russ said, carefully putting aside his brushes and paint rags, freeing his hands. He stood tense and poised, ready for the slightest opportunity to jump the madman.

"Bitches, all of 'em. Mom warned me! They'll play around on you. Every damned one of 'em! Alanna was just like the rest. They'll cut your heart out, if you don't cut theirs out first!" Kyle suddenly shrieked with laughter, and the knife pressed a bit more tightly against Holly's neck.

She gasped in reaction, and Russ's eyes widened in fear. But he didn't reveal that fear in his words. Still speaking calmly, he said, "Kyle, let her go. It's me you want, isn't it? So let's have it out. Right here and now."

A sacrificial offering. He was willing to put his very life on the line to take Kyle's attention away from Holly. She read a silent plea in the artist's gaze: *If he moves away from you, lowers the knife even a fraction, make a break for it.*

"No!" Kyle screamed. "I want you *both*. She's going to be the latest victim of the Butcher Knife Murderer. Only she'll put up a lot of fight before she goes down. Maybe even kill her attacker, eh, Russ?"

The publisher was frenzied, his eyes brilliant and glittering in the glow of the artist's work lamps. Involuntarily, Holly thought of Ivor Wilcox's notes. Madness mixed with cold calculation. Carefully plotting—until the final, manic moments of his crimes. A repressed sexual murderer . . .

Mom warned me . . . bitches, all of them . . . cut your heart out . . .

The incident at the picnic must have been sheer impulse, a variation on Kyle's usual killings. But now he had returned full force to his "normal" pattern.

"Alanna," Russ said, his face twisting with rage. "You killed her, you bastard," and he sidled forward a step.

Instantly, the knife dug into Holly's skin. "Careful, or you'll see her die right here and now." Kyle's manner had become that of a giant cat playing with two helpless mice. "Oh, yeah! Alanna got it from me, and good. The lying little bitch. Come on, Russ. Crawl. I like to hear 'em tell me how they'll do anything I ask, only please, please don't kill 'em!" She felt his powerful frame shaking with insane laughter. The blade quivered at her throat.

Russ's eyes were lasers, burning with rage at this insane predator who had invaded his studio. Holly could all but hear wheels turning in the artist's quick brain. She longed desperately to help him subdue this madman before they were both killed. But how?

As Kyle's laughter started to dwindle, Russ spat a word.

Holly had heard the term used lightly, as part of rough, masculine banter. This was light-years away from that. It was not just a crude obscenity but a specific accusation of incest.

With an incoherent roar, Kyle let go of Holly and lunged at Russ.

The men collided like rampaging beasts, knocking over the easel and smashing the lamps, plunging the studio into near darkness. Holly was hurled aside, skidding helplessly across the uncarpeted floor.

In the dim light she saw Russ gripping Kyle's knife hand, holding the blade arrested scant inches from his throat. The pair grappled violently, grunting and snarling curses, twisting this way and that.

Holly thought frantically. What had Russ said? If anyone broke in, club him with one of those long guns hanging on the wall.

She tried to crawl around the combatants, dodging their feet as the men struggled wildly, kicking and wheeling. At any moment, they'd fall on her! And they were blocking her access to the guns!

Russ was fighting bravely, but Kyle was the heavier of the two, possibly canceling Russ's advantage in height.

And Kyle was an experienced killer. He'd done this before! If he couldn't be stopped, she and Russ would be added to the body count!

How stupid she'd been! Russ's pistol! The gun on his bedside table! He'd said that he kept it there at all times as burglar protection.

Right now they needed protection from something far, far worse than a burglar!

Seeing a momentary opening, Holly scrambled past the men and ran toward the loft. The only illumination in the studio now came from the large north window, and that glow was fading fast. It provided barely enough light for her to see where she was going. She stumbled, banging into the stair's newel post, and, on her hands and knees, she clawed her way upward like a terror-stricken child.

When she reached the loft, she flailed about blindly, barking her shins on furniture and half falling over the bed. Groping for the table. Dragging open its drawer.

Behind and below her, animalistic grunting mingled with crashing sounds and the noises of bodies impacting wood.

Holly's fingers closed around the gun's butt. She lifted it

and whirled, hurrying to the head of the stairs, peering down into the darkened studio.

The crashing noises had stopped. Only one figure stood upright, dimly visible against the window.

A man's silhouette, advancing on the steps, coming for her.

"Russ?" she cried hopefully, then caught her breath as the approaching figure raised its right hand. A hand holding a knife.

Just like her nightmare!

Kyle.

Where was Russ? Was he hurt, or . . . ?

"Don't come any closer!" Holly screamed, pointing the gun.

The killer's form was shrouded in darkness, exactly as in her terrible dream. He came on ponderously, one step at a time.

"I'm warning you! I'll shoot!" Holly tried desperately to remember everything Russ had taught her. She lined up the sights and pulled the trigger. Nothing happened.

Kyle's laughter was a hideous shriek, lancing at her ears. He'd hesitated on the third or fourth step when she pointed the gun. But now he was coming forward again, cackling with contempt.

"You stay right there, baby. I'll take good care of you . . ."

Of course! She'd forgotten Russ's instructions. First cock the hammer, then pull the trigger. Line up the sights, inhale, pull.

There was a stupendous roar. She rocked backwards as much in reaction to the noise as the weapon's recoil. Russ had warned her she'd been firing special light loads when they were target shooting. *This* was the real thing.

Kyle gave a queer sort of smothered squawk and fell sideways off the stairs.

The knife spun out of his grasp, clattering away into the darkness. In the last glow of twilight, she saw him scramble toward the screen door, trying to get to his feet. His left arm dangled limply, and he clutched it with his right hand.

"Nooooo!"

He was howling. The cry was barely human.

Holly aimed the gun again, just in case. She vowed to sell her life and Russ's dearly if that monster came for them again.

But Kyle didn't turn. Staggering like a drunk, he reeled through the open door, almost tearing the screen off its hinges.

Limp, trembling with adrenaline-induced fright, Holly made her way down the stairs and searched for the light switch. As an overhead fixture came on, she groaned. Russ was propped against the wall. He winced, shaking his head. Blood trickled from his scalp. His hand pressed a spot high on his chest, near his left shoulder, and a thin line of blood seeped between his fingers.

"Oh, no!" Holly cried, dropping down beside him. He blinked at her for a heartbeat or two. Then his eyes widened and he reached out and took the gun away from her.

"Watch that. It's cocked," he said, and corrected whatever she'd left undone with the weapon. "Bastard knocked me into the wall, laid my head open . . ."

"I . . . I shot him." Belatedly, Holly was shocked by her own actions.

"Good girl," Russ muttered.

As she tried to examine his wound, he complained grumpily. Then both of them tensed as there was the crunch of tires on the driveway.

They could still hear Kyle's hysterical baying, but that was fading.

Much closer, an assortment of voices babbled questions. Despite Holly's protests, Russ levered his way upright. Still holding the gun, he moved unsteadily toward the door. She snatched a box of antiseptic tissues from the bathroom and hurriedly dogged his tracks, afraid he was doing himself further injury with these exertions.

Maud's mammoth car sat in the driveway. She, Toby, and Ivor stood beside the vehicle, staring at the hiking trail. As Russ and Holly approached they heard Maud exclaiming, "Forgetting your speech at the club was bad enough, Ivor, but what the hell was *that* all about?" and she pointed along the path.

"Did you see Kyle?" Russ demanded, panting to a halt. "Where did he go?"

"Not in his car, for sure," Ivor answered. "I guess we blocked him in when we arrived. He went running that way. Hey, man! You're cut!"

Holly slipped a compress of the sterile tissues inside Russ's shirt and mopped at his head wound. He waved a blood-smeared hand irritably. "Never mind about that now. We've got to catch him." The artist explained to the others, "Kyle just tried to kill us. He's the Butcher Knife Murderer."

Toby crumpled across a fender, hammering his fists on the metal. "Damn! I knew it! I just knew it. Damn, damn, damn!" He wailed like a man whose worst fears had been realized. Ivor was torn, unable to decide whether to help Toby or Russ.

"Well, if that isn't the limit!" Maud said, whistling. "Who'd have dreamed? We saw a rental with out-of-state plates parked over there by the bushes and thought—'that's kinda weird.' Then Kyle came out of nowhere, screaming like crazy, and ran himself right onto the hood of my car. Hit so hard he bounced. After that, he galloped off east on the trail. I think he was bleeding," she added.

"Not from ramming your car," Russ assured her. "Holly shot him with my .38."

"Son of a bitch," Ivor said with admiration. "Sure looked to me like his arm was broke. But he wasn't actin' hurt. Not exactly. Just . . . well, he was practically frothing at the mouth. Maybe 'cause he couldn't get to his wheels."

Russ was wobbling, and Holly put an arm around him. These people were supposed to be his friends. Couldn't they see that he needed a doctor? She started to make that point, but he cut her off.

"I doubt if he *is* hurting—yet. It'll take a while for the shock to wear off. But we have to track him down. Can't let him run around and kill someone else—"

"I know where he's gone," Holly said suddenly, surprised at her own certainty.

The artist looked at her and allowed himself a weak smile. "So do I. Let's go. Ivor, get on your cell phone and call the cops. And . . . take care of Toby."

The little computer tech straightened, wiping his face. "I'm okay, now. Really."

Russ took a step toward the footpath, ignoring Holly's attempts to dissuade him, but stolidly accepting her supporting arm. Maud brought them both to their senses. "For Pete's sake, don't be idiots. If you're bound and determined to chase him, get in the car. I'll take you wherever you're going."

"Please," Holly begged. Grudgingly, Russ acquiesced, muttering that he'd bloody up Maud's land yacht. After a bit of resistance, though, he allowed the others to assist him into the vehicle.

As Maud put her car in gear, she asked, "Just where are we going?"

"To Sylvia's," Holly and Russ replied in unison.

Dark Lake's den mother sucked in an astonished breath but followed orders. A scant few minutes later, she pulled to a stop at the Preis's ranch houses. Although visibly shaky, Russ was stubbornly set on seeing these matters through to their conclusion. As they emerged from the car, Holly glanced at the gun he still held, worrying. Did he intend to seek his own form of revenge for Alanna's death?

The group heard loud music behind the houses. Walking around to the lakeside lawn, they found Sylvia lying on a chaise lounge, a pitcher of martinis and a blaring radio by her side. The publisher's bikini was brief enough to earn an indecency citation.

"He's not here yet, I see," Russ growled. He snapped off the radio.

Sylvia sat bolt upright in astonishment. "What the hell do you think you're doing?" Then she saw the blood on his shirt. Blue patio lights turned the stain a ghastly color. She gaped at the intruders. "Why . . . Russ, Maud . . . what . . . ?"

"I've been stabbed, thanks to your precious son," Russ snarled. He tried to stand up straight, but couldn't help swaying a bit. "Good thing I rolled with the blow, or he'd have killed me. Just like he killed Alanna and those other women, and would have killed Holly."

"You . . . you're crazy!" Sylvia retorted with a shaky laugh. "You've flipped out completely! Since Holly stood him up, Kyle went to Chicago with a cute little—"

"He's not there, Sylvia," Maud said. She no longer sounded like the jolly mother hen. Her friendly face was drawn in soft grief. "He came tearing out of Russ's a few minutes ago. I saw him, and so did Toby and Ivor. And believe me, Kyle was definitely a man running away from some serious sins."

"Ridiculous!" The hard-faced publisher leapt to her feet, spilling her drink. She moved forward as though she meant to scratch out Maud's eyes.

And then there was a thrashing sound in the hedge, very close to the lake. Sylvia seemed to take root, only her eyes turning in the direction of the disturbance. The others looked that way, too.

It was almost a mile from Russ's studio to the Preis's houses. Kyle apparently had run all the way, bleeding and frantic, his fragile hold on sanity in tatters.

Like an intoxicated puppet, he flailed toward the group, falling again and again, squealing with pain, then climbing to his feet and reeling forward once more. Until finally he was confronting Sylvia. Plainly, he was unaware anyone else was present. Sylvia, her harridan's face a mess, gawped at him in disbelief.

"You! You said it would be so simple!" Kyle yelled, gulping air greedily, his chest heaving. His left arm hung useless. Holly shuddered and glanced away when she saw the damage her moment of bravery had inflicted. "All you! Ever since I can remember. You! Telling me what to do . . ."

"B . . . baby!" Sylvia's voice was an echo from purgatory. "What did they do to you?"

"They? You! All you. I did it for *you!* Alanna and Gloria and Ella and Francine and the rest. Nothing to me. But you said they'd . . . you said . . . you wouldn't love me unless I gave them what they had coming. *You!*" As he had at the picnic, he began to chant, over and over, "Goddammit, goddammit!"

Then he struck out with his good right hand, his strong fingers closing about Sylvia's throat. Her shriek of fear ended in a sick gargle, and her long red nails clawed at him futilely.

Russ pointed the pistol at the madman's head. "Let go of her, Kyle. I mean it. Haven't you done enough killing for one lifetime?"

The young publisher's face was streaked with tears. His rage melted into childish confusion as he stared at the gun. Gradually, his fingers relaxed. Sylvia, choking and sobbing, dropped at his feet.

In a cold, level tone Russ said, "It's a damned heavy temptation to put a bullet through you anyway. But you don't deserve that kind of mercy. You didn't give any to Alanna or the others. Now just back off. We'll all stay right here and wait for the police. It's over Kyle. All over."

Whimpering, Kyle fell to his knees. He moaned, rocking back and forth, cradling his injured arm. "Hurts," he cried. "Hurts so bad. Didn't mean to . . . until she told me . . . told me that Daddy said I didn't have any guts . . . ."

Holly closed her eyes, nauseated by the implications in that revelation. She suspected an investigation would show that Kyle's father was yet another victim of this deadly mother-son relationship.

Russ slowly lowered the revolver to his side, staring morosely at the pair. Plainly, he felt no triumph, only grim satisfaction that at last the truth was known. Soon, Holly would absolutely insist that he sit down. He couldn't continue to ignore that knife wound and other hurts he'd suffered in the brawl. But for the moment, she said nothing.

Alanna, avenged, but not in a way that anyone anticipated. Her killer—rather her killers—finally had been exposed. Sylvia's manipulative behavior and evil scheming had reaped a terrible harvest. And Kyle was utterly broken, bereft even of sanity.

Sylvia knelt beside her son, pressing his head against her breast. As if he were an infant, she began to croon, her tears

201

mingling with his. "It's all right, baby. Mommy's here. I'll take care of everything. You just do what Mommy says. You be a good boy, now, a good boy . . ."

Holly touched Russ's good arm and studied his face. He heaved a sigh. "I guess I don't want to kill him after all," the artist said tiredly. "Not any more. I can even feel a bit sorry for him, and for her. But only a very little bit." Sirens wailed in the distance, approaching fast. Russ cocked his head toward the sound and managed a slight smile. "And *this* time, I'm going to be glad to see the police."

Chapter 12

Russ carefully lowered himself onto the sofa amid the semicircle of chairs facing Scorpio House's dramatic fireplace. For once, he didn't begrudge help, and he murmured his thanks as Bianca placed a supportive pillow at his back. Holly eased herself down beside him.

"Better?" she said anxiously. "Stitches still hurt?"

"I'm okay as long as I don't move too fast, or stretch the wrong way. And I didn't appreciate that crack from your friendly, local resident, either. 'It must be true love if you're sharing the same emergency room.' Bah!"

With a laugh, Holly said, "You must admit that between my ankle and your wounds we've provided him with plenty of business lately." She didn't push the teasing any further, though.

At this point, she could even look back with amusement on Bianca's flare of anger in the emergency room. The trigger was a minor disagreement with Stephen over their medical insurance. A trivial thing. Yet Bianca had given up the argument quickly and with remarkable grace. That seemed like further evidence of Stephen's growing success in taming and channeling his wife's capricious nature.

Holly listened to the others rehashing recent events. It was almost like hearing an account of something that happened to someone else, far away and long ago.

Ivor was saying, "Man, I guess we all were pretty dense— me most of all. There I had all the stuff right in front of me in my files. And dumb me, I couldn't pull it together. All my jabber about Jack the Ripper and repressed sexuality . . . dead tip-off, if I'd only used my head."

Holly couldn't help feeling Ivor's mental lapse wasn't nearly as great as her own. How many times had Kyle's castles-in-air chatter and twitchy mannerisms reminded her of her late father's aberrations? And the clues pointing to *Sylvia!* With her training and background, Holly Frey, of all people, ought to have spotted those tell-tale signs of serious abnormality.

". . . yes, I'm afraid Kyle is a tragic example of western node imbalance," Stephen was explaining. "At least by my analysis. A really fine mind twisted by malefic influences. You heard the police captain call Kyle a masterful amateur psychologist? He knew his rigged recording would bring Holly running to help Russ. What a brain. If that boy had only turned it to constructive purposes—"

"He tried to, from his point of view," Holly said.

Russ spoke up, "I talk too damned much, which didn't help. If I hadn't run off at the mouth while Kyle was visiting my studio, he wouldn't have been able to tape my voice. I never realized he was using one of those super miniaturized gadgets. I gave him just about everything he needed to serve us both up on a plate. Must have been kid's play for him to patch together that fake phone call that nearly got us killed."

"No, it wasn't your fault," Toby said suddenly. The little man had a trifle more color in his face now than he had earlier. With sympathy, they had listened then as he'd filled in all the technical blanks for an interviewing police officer. Few people knew as much about the gadgets Russ mentioned as Toby did. "I showed him how. The works. What he didn't get from me, he pried out of some of his golfing buddies in the telecom field. But I started him off, taught him the ropes—"

"You didn't teach him how to kill," Maud cut in. "That was his own idea, and hers."

"Yeah, man, quit blamin' yourself," Ivor said soberly, laying a comforting hand on Toby's shoulder.

A pained smile tugged at the computer tech's mouth. "But I ought to have known, deep down, that the potential was there. I'd seen it in him, heard Stephen talking about the bad signs . . . and I didn't tell anybody." Toby shuddered and covered his face with his hands. Ivor shook him gently, chidingly, his dark face taut with concern. Still feeling guilty, Toby went on, "I knew, subconsciously. I'm responsible—"

"The police don't think so," Stephen told him. The astrologer looked tired. Holly knew, now, how much he tried to share other people's burdens. And she'd seen his reaction while police questioned Kyle and Sylvia. If he could have, Stephen would have helped *them*. He steepled his forefingers and continued, "According to the detectives, until this overt attack, there was really no evidence pointing to Kyle and his mother. They covered their tracks far too well. Even if you'd told the police your suspicions, they would merely have thanked you for your input. There was no proof. It would have been your word against Kyle's."

Holly added her weight to Stephen's reassurances. "I should have guessed the truth myself, long before tonight. I'd been in his offices, seen all his super-modern computer equipment, that separate door to his suite, the unattended parking garage. For someone with Kyle's skills, it all must have been easy."

"Yeah, easy," Russ said, his voice harsh. "Like the cops said, we know, now, that Kyle's secretary wasn't hearing *him*, only a recording, the night Alanna was killed. He and Sylvia had even set up a phony credit card account. Somehow they fixed it so Kyle could get a rental car any time he needed, with no way to trace it back to him, or to her. Just like that night. He drove hell-bent out to Dark Lake, murdered Alanna, and returned to Preis Enterprises without anybody but Sylvia knowing he'd been gone. Slick as hell. About what I might have expected from those two."

"Perfect alibis," Holly agreed. "Every time. Between them, they must have believed they could outwit anyone."

"They wouldn't have outwitted the stockholders, not much longer," Stephen said. The others regarded him curiously as he explained, "New financial problems had turned up recently. Extremely serious ones. So serious I was again considering changing my publisher. Dan Preis had talked me out of that once. And in retrospect I wonder if he wasn't conducting his own internal investigation into root causes . . ."

"Sylvia," Holly guessed.

Her brother-in-law nodded. "Quite possibly. After Dan died, it seemed unkind to press the inquiry. Technically, it wasn't my concern. Anyway, finances *did* improve."

"Insurance will do marvels," Ivor said, his cynicism solid enough to walk on.

"That may well have been behind it all," Stephen said solemnly. "As disgusting as it is to think about. Perhaps a renewed police inquiry—and Sylvia's confession—will clear up that mystery. At any rate, it does seem as if I will be changing publishers after all. Poor Dan. I hope he didn't suffer in that accident—"

"Accident?" the writer challenged, snorting. "Hah! The cops and insurance people always figured there was something screwy there. But like the Butcher Knife murders, until Kyle totally lost control, there was no proof. If he hadn't gone over the edge . . . I'll be interested to find out what really set him off in the first place."

Shadow Over Scorpio

"We can speculate." Stephen's words were heavy with sadness.

Other words rang clear in Holly's memory: *Until she told me that Daddy said I didn't have any guts . . ."*

Sylvia, the ruthless manipulator, using her own son's madness to eliminate her troublesome husband when Dan Preis started to get suspicious!

What a waste! Kyle's intelligence and charm, wielded as a deadly weapon! Sylvia had aimed the young man much as Holly had aimed Russ's gun. Guiding and goading, Sylvia taught Kyle to work together with her, plotting every detail of the murders. Even down to things like that rental car Kyle had taken to Russ's studio. His own vehicle was probably still parked in the garage in Chicago, calculated proof that he was far away when these latest murders would have taken place!

And his poor secretary! How was she going to feel when the police explained all of this to her? She'd been his unwitting alibi, probably a number of times. Perhaps she, like Toby, had suspected something. But Kyle could charm the toenails off a dragon when he tried. The secretary had remained loyal to the very end, no doubt convincing herself that sweet, handsome Kyle Preis couldn't possibly do anything so awful. Surely *he* couldn't be a killer!

"I should have told somebody," Toby said, still flogging himself with guilt.

"And been killed yourself?" Maud said. "Honey, he would have finished you off like all the rest, if he'd thought you were going to get in his way. No, no, you're not to blame."

"Maybe fate is," Holly murmured, "for making Kyle what he was, and for making Sylvia his mother."

Russ's hand reached for hers. "If I'd known he was the one who tried to drown you, I would have killed him then and there."

207

"Well, I wasn't even sure it was a man in the water with me, not until tonight. It might even have been you," she said, chuckling at his startled expression. "For that matter, it might have been you chasing me in the storm. Or Stephen. Or any of a dozen people. I never saw who it was, in or out of that rowboat. And it's just as far across the lake from your place as it is from the Preis properties. In fact, considering the fact that Kyle set things up so everyone believed he was at a golf tournament—and I *knew* I'd left you at the studio—logic demands that if I suspected anyone, it would have been you."

"But it wasn't," he countered with a smirk. She reflected that he was mellowing fast. He didn't seem to mind her teasing.

Ivor broke in, "I hate to sound callous, but this will mean plenty of free publicity for my book. And think of the finale I can write now. You'll be famous before I get through, Russ, Holly." Before either of them could protest that they preferred anonymity, he rushed on, "Think o' that! Already had it down in my notes about the Butcher Knife Murderer plotting everything out cold when he started cuttin' to get his jollies. And he worked it out like a rocket launch, down to the last detail. Even like checkin' to see if Holly was going to be alone in the house tonight."

"He didn't always plan," she corrected him. Something about the writer's enthusiasm made her want to puncture his balloon. "I don't think he planned what happened at the picnic. He didn't have a knife, remember? It was sheer impulse. I think it was because Sylvia pushed him over the edge that night."

"She'd push anyone over the line," Bianca agreed as she and Melanie trotted in, bearing laden trays. "I think we all need a little comfort food and drink after what we've been through."

"No alcohol for Russ," Holly said quickly, eyeing the bottles her sister was setting out. "Not mixed with those painkillers the doctor gave him."

"Maud, she's usurping your mother hen job," Russ complained, but his pale eyes sparkled with amusement. "It's okay. She's right, Bianca. Any more dope, or alcohol, and I'll pass out," he said. A thick layer of bandages peeped whitely through the cut in his shirt and stitches on his brow glistened with spray antiseptic. "Whatever the doc put in that hypo was sure good stuff. But I'm going to be sore as hell in the morning, and have one wowser of a headache."

"Thank God that will be the only aftereffect," Maud said.

Toby mumbled something that sounded like, "I'll drink to that," chug-a-lugging the contents of his glass.

"For us, at least," Bianca said, her gaze meeting Holly's. "Are you all right? I know how much you can empathize."

A proud, doting smile crossed the astrologer's face. "Brava, my love! She *is* thinking about Kyle and Sylvia. How astute of you to sense that!"

Holly took her time before speaking. "Yes, I am sorry for them, in a way. But I'm far *more* sorry for those they killed. That pair must be locked away where they can't hurt anyone ever again!"

Stephen turned his glass around and around between his long fingers. "It's such a pity I can't keep constant tabs on my clients. After the fact, I checked, and when I saw the current position of Sylvia's Mars, and all the other malign influences, well . . . !"

"Look, I made sandwiches, too," Bianca said, seizing the chance to turn the conversation away from that subject.

Maud joined in the game. "Oh, goodie! Mm! Ham! My favorite!" she cried, pouncing. The others laughed, Toby loudest of all, which Holly was happy to see. He seemed to be recuperating from his bout of guilt. Complete recovery would take time. She knew that he had, in a way, loved Kyle, and learning the truth had hurt the computer tech badly. But with Ivor present to occupy his affections, she was sure he'd come out of it in fine shape.

Stephen leaned forward, eyeing her intently. "No more thoughts of menace from Scorpio, now," he chided.

She nodded in fervent agreement. All that was in the past, something she could look back on without fear. "And no more hair-raising prognostications from you! About how I must be at Scorpio House when unspecified and terrible events occur," Holly said, shaking a finger at him in mock reproach. "As it certainly did. If I'd stayed in Norris Falls—"

"You'd never have met me," Russ interrupted, his smile positively lecherous.

Stephen guffawed. Then the astrologer laid his hands on Russ's and Holly's, like a priest blessing a couple standing before his altar. "Trust me, my young friends, the portents from this point on are very good indeed."

With that, he moved toward Bianca, slipping an arm around her waist, snuggling close enough that she had to set down a tray before she dropped it.

Russ studied them thoughtfully, asking Holly, "What was that last remark all about?"

"I'll tell you—sometime."

"There you go again! What's the deep, dark secret when you smile like that? You're my own private version of the Mona Lisa."

Her silly little smile, that Bianca called "all knowing," claiming it intrigued men. For once, it appeared big sister was right.

"Well, I am an Aquarian. Take a good look at the painting in my room. You painted it, after all, and if you don't know an

Aquarian smile when you see it, who does?" Holly demanded. Russ frowned, obviously trying to recall the picture. He *had* painted quite a few since that one left his easel, and it was doubtful he could remember every piece of artwork he'd ever done. She went on, "Come to that, if we're going to nit-pick each other, I want to warn you—never again stare at a woman the way you stared at me that night at the Martins'."

"Stare? Me?"

"You. Holes through me. Like you were trying to hypno-tize me, or seduce me."

"That's not a bad idea," he said, his lips brushing her cheek. He winced as the movement pulled at stitches and his barely closed wounds. "Ouch! Well, maybe not just yet. But when I heal up, watch out, Mona Lisa."

"Scorpio," Holly said absently. Russ looked quizzical. "Oh, I was just thinking about things Stephen and I once dis-cussed. About one of my dreams. I was afraid of the sign of Scorpio. But as you pointed out, if I'd never come to Scorpio House, I'd never have met you. And Bianca would still be trying to take care of her dowdy sister."

"I think you take care of yourself very well," he said, grin-ning. "Damned sure thing—I won't ever get out of line with *you*. Not since I taught you how to shoot!"

"Oh? Was that what you were going to say that afternoon? When we were target shooting? You said you wanted to tell me something, but then you got that call from Baskins, and you never finished the sentence."

"Didn't I?" Russ said innocently. His eyes weren't fiery, now. They were soft with love. "I guess I planned to tell you—not that I believe any of this astrology crap—that your horoscope and mine match. According to his philosophy, we ought to be in for all kinds of good stuff, right? Cancels out that nonsense about my 'having a Scorpio Moon,' huh?"

She let him draw her into the crook of his good arm. He was favoring his wounds, yet insisting on being close. On touching. Smiling up at Russ, she said, "Okay. Let's admit it—our fate must have been written in our stars."

About the Author

Juanita Coulson's first novel—a Western—was written at age eleven. It received a kind rejection from an amused Scribner's editor. Her next attempt at professional publication, in 1963, was a collaboration with her friend and mentor, Marion Zimmer Bradley. That one *did* sell, and was followed by sixteen novels and an assortment of genre short stories and nonfiction. As co-creator with her late husband, Robert "Buck" Coulson, she was awarded science fiction's Hugo for *Yandro*, Best Amateur Publication of 1965. A native Hoosier, she currently resides in London, Ohio, near Columbus.